I0540942

Luke's Temptation

By

Cara Marsi

Luke's Temptation
Copyright © 2014 Carolyn Matkowsky

Print ISBN: 978-0-9915975-3-6
Kindle ASIN: B00MYC97LU

ALL RIGHTS RESERVED. With the exception of quotes used in reviews, this book may not be reproduced or used in whole or in part by any means existing without written permission from Carolyn Matkowsky.
Published by The Painted Lady Press
United States of America
This book is a work of fiction and all characters exist solely in the author's imagination. Any resemblance to persons, living or dead, is purely coincidental. Any references to places, events or locales are used in a fictitious manner.
Cover by Harris Channing
Formatting by Aileen Fish

Acknowledgements

Thank you to my critique partners, Judythe, Sue, and Tessy, for their advice and suggestions that helped make *Luke's Temptation* a better story.

A special thanks to Ann Whitaker, friend, talented author, and English teacher for her editing help.

Danger and desire brew a volatile mix as two wounded souls fight to stay alive and find love.

Anita Santisi is an independent, successful businesswoman with a wounded heart. And some very bad people after her. Break-ins, home invasions, and attempted abductions have turned her comfortable life dangerous. Can she trust her mysterious, sexy new neighbor, Luke Corrado, or is he behind the criminal acts?

Special Agent Luke Corrado carries his guilt like a loaded Glock. A woman he loved was murdered because of him. Now, on a new undercover assignment to protect Anita Santisi, he's determined to redeem himself. What he doesn't expect is that Anita will tempt him to let down the barriers around his heart.

As Anita and Luke find themselves in ever-increasing danger, they must fight to stay alive. Will they open their hearts to each other before it's too late?

CHAPTER ONE

Anita Santisi locked her car with her remote and juggled her packages as she strode toward her condo loft in an upscale suburb of Philadelphia. With the street lights illuminating her way in the darkness, she struggled to hold onto her packages and picked her way up the steep steps in her stiletto boots.

"Why the heck did I buy so many Christmas gifts?" she muttered. But she knew. She loved buying baby clothes and toys for her cousins' babies. And as honorary aunt, it was her duty to spoil them.

She got to her front door and let out a small cry. Her insides shook. The packages fell from her hands to land in a pile by her feet. Her front door hung open on its hinges with a huge hole at the bottom as if someone had kicked it in with heavy boots.

She did a quick scan of the area. No one else was around. Forcing air into lungs that felt ready to burst, she turned and ran down the steps, stumbling in her haste. Grabbing the handrail, she caught herself. On unsteady legs, she gripped the railing and hurried the rest of the way down. Near the bottom, she lost her balance and almost fell, but strong arms grabbed her and kept her upright.

"What's wrong?" a male voice asked.

She screamed and tore loose from the stranger. When she looked up into deep brown eyes, almost black in their intensity, her heart rate kicked up a notch. Had he been walking along the sidewalk, or did he follow her from her house?

Gulping breaths, she backed away. Her attention on the

stranger, she pulled her phone out of her purse. With shaking fingers, she dialed 911. When the operator answered, Anita said, "My home's been broken into. The intruder might still be inside."

With a promise the police were on their way and an admonition from the operator not to go into her house, Anita disconnected. Still clutching her phone, she put more distance between her and the tall stranger.

"Your house was broken into?" he asked. "I'm sorry. I'll stay with you and wait for the police."

"They'll be here any minute. I'm fine now. You can leave." She licked her lips, and not taking her eyes off the stranger, she fished in her purse for her car's remote. It had a panic button. If he dared move toward her, she'd set it off.

He nodded toward the adjoining condos. "I don't see how I can leave since I live here."

She swallowed. "Live here?"

"I'm your new neighbor. I thought this was a safe neighborhood."

"Neighbor?" Trying to wrap her mind around that surprising information, words failed her and she could only continue to stare up at him. Her loft, in a restored warehouse, was one of two condos that shared a common wall. Each had a private entrance, the doors a few feet from each other. The loft next to hers had stood empty the past year since the owner transferred to Japan for his work. She'd heard someone rented it recently.

Her alleged new neighbor furrowed his brow. "You okay?"

Fairly sure he wasn't her intruder or an ax murderer, Anita still had to be cautious. She put her finger over the panic button on her remote.

"I'm Luke Corrado." He held out his hand. "This is a hell of a way to meet."

"It sure is. I'm Anita Santisi." She decided caution trumped politeness and didn't take the proffered hand. Still on guard in case he made a movement toward her, she looked more closely at him. He was easy on the eyes, with his short black hair and those dark eyes that watched her as if he thought her the most fascinating woman he'd ever met. She'd noticed a dimple in his cheek when he smiled. Nice lips, not too thin, not too full, just right for kissing. Smooth olive skin stretched taut over high cheekbones, inviting her to touch.

"Like what you see?" he asked, showing that dimple again.

Heat suffused her face. He might be eye candy, but he was arrogant. Anita didn't tolerate arrogant men. And she still didn't trust him. She sent him a look she'd perfected, one that usually sent grown men scrambling for cover. Apparently, it wasn't sending this man anywhere. He looked contrite, or tried to look contrite.

"I'm sorry," he said. "That didn't come out right. I sounded like a jerk."

"Yeah, you did."

He gave her that dimpled smile that made warmth swirl through her despite her anxiety and the late November chill.

His magnetism tempted her to scan the rest of him. His black leather jacket and black sweater didn't disguise the width of his shoulders or the breadth of his chest. Close-fitting jeans hugged long legs that seemed to go on forever. All in all, one hot package.

"Let's start over. I'm your new neighbor, Luke Corrado."

Before she could respond, lights flashed in the darkness as three police cars pulled up to the curb.

◇◇◇

Her place was in shambles. The intruder or intruders had slit the cushions on her leather sofa and chairs in the living area and tossed the contents of her kitchen drawers and cabinets onto the tiled floor. Her bedroom was in worse shape. They'd torn off her bedclothes, shifted the mattress till it perched precariously on the bed, and emptied her bureau drawers and closet. Her shoeboxes were opened and her shoes tossed everywhere.

Fighting tears, Anita stood in her wrecked condo while the police dusted for fingerprints. They'd taken her statement, and now her new neighbor was in the kitchen giving his statement to the detective. He'd shown the police his key and identification proving he lived in the condo next door.

Needing the comforting presence of family, Anita had called her cousin Franco Callahan, owner of an international construction company. His wife, Jo Fortune, was a security expert who'd recently started her own firm with Harris, a former SEAL.

A commotion at the front door caught Anita's attention. A burly cop standing guard attempted to keep Jo and Franco from entering.

"We're family. Let us in," Franco said as he pushed past the cop.

"It's okay. Please let them in." Anita rushed to the door.

"Anita, this is terrible." Jo enfolded her in a bear hug.

Franco rubbed his hand up and down Anita's back. "Are you okay?"

Anita nodded.

Jo released her and stepped back. "That's the most important thing, that you're okay."

"What did they take?" Franco asked.

Anita balled her hands at her sides fighting for calm. "Nothing that I can tell yet."

"Strange," Franco said.

"I'll get you some water." Jo started for the kitchen, but stopped, her eyes wide, as Luke Corrado strode toward her.

He held a large glass filled with ice water. With a smile, he handed it to Anita. "Drink this. Are you feeling better?"

Anita nodded. "Thanks." As if he held out a lifeline, she took the glass from him and wrapped her hands around it.

Luke, Jo and Franco stared at each other.

"Sorry," Anita said. "Luke Corrado, my cousin Franco Callahan and his wife Jo Fortune Callahan."

As Luke shook hands with Jo and Franco, Anita sipped the water. The cooling liquid wound its way smoothly down her throat. She wished it could cleanse the dirtiness she felt that someone had violated her house, had violated her.

Jo and Franco were quietly watching Luke.

"Luke rented the place next to mine." Feeling uncomfortable at the continued silence from the others, Anita said, "Jo, you didn't have to come with Franco. You need to stay home and rest."

Franco put his arm around his wife. "Jo? Rest? Not my little dynamo."

Jo patted her baby bump. "Not so little anymore."

"But still beautiful." He kissed her on the cheek.

A twinge of regret wound through Anita. She'd long ago given up the dream of finding love, of happily-ever-after. Once she thought she'd found it, but it had all been an illusion.

Luke stepped away from the group. "Now that your family's here, I guess I'd better go."

"Thanks for your help," Anita said.

"Nice to meet you," Jo and Franco said in unison as Luke headed toward the door.

Raising one eyebrow, Jo looked at Anita.

"What?" Anita said. "He's a neighbor."

Jo chuckled. "Okay."

Ignoring Jo's grin, Anita sipped more water, her thoughts on her new neighbor. While the police were searching the house, Luke had told her he was single and lived alone. Interest had flared in her, but she'd smothered it. Her luck with men sucked. The last guy she'd dated went out of town on business two months ago and never came back.

The detective walked up to her and shut his notebook, slipping it into his pocket. "We need you to come down to the station tomorrow so we can get your fingerprints for elimination purposes."

"I'll be there."

"You're sure nothing was taken?" he asked.

She nodded. "All my jewelry seems to be accounted for. My computer and tablet are here. I'll look around more later and let you know if anything's missing."

"Please do." He frowned. "Is there anything the thieves might have been looking for, other than the usual jewels and electronics? Anything you might have they'd want? A large amount of cash?"

"No, I don't leave cash around the house. I own a salon, but I have nothing special anyone would want."

"They might think you keep money here. We've had a rash of home invasions against business owners." He shot her a wry smile. "It's the holiday season. The crooks need money to go Christmas shopping."

"I'm just glad I wasn't here when they broke in."

"We're glad, too," Franco said. He looked at the detective. "Are you done? We'd like to get that door fixed as soon as possible."

"We're done." The detective pulled a card from his jacket pocket and handed it to Anita. "If you find that items were stolen, or anything else occurs to you, call me."

Anita took the card from him and slipped it into her pants pocket. "Thanks, detective."

"We'll be out of your way. I wouldn't recommend spending the night here."

When the police left, Jo touched Anita's arm. "You're coming home with us."

"I can't leave my house unsecured like this."

"Taken care of," Franco said. "On the way here, I called Harris. He's sending someone over to watch the house tonight, and I've arranged for a few of my men to replace that door first thing in the morning. I'll call in some favors and get you a new sofa and chairs right away." He rubbed his hands together. "Pack a bag. You're coming with us. And none of that Santisi stubbornness."

"Harris arranged for the alarm company to install a security system in the morning, too," Jo said.

Frowning, Franco looked at Anita. "Are you sure there's no money hidden anywhere? Maybe the previous owners hid something."

Anita shook her head. "After two years of extensive renovations, if there was any money hidden, we would have found it by now." She would rather the intruders be simply thieves looking for jewelry to sell for drugs. The thought that something more

sinister was behind the break-in sent chills down her spine.

Franco glanced at his watch. "We need to get going."

"I'll help you pack." Jo said. As the women walked up the stairs to the bedroom, Jo said, "Your new neighbor is hot."

Anita snorted. "I don't care how hot he is, I'm off men for now."

◇◇◇

Luke used his secure cell phone to place a call. Murray answered on the first ring.

"Corrado, did you make contact?"

"Yeah. She literally fell into my arms. I waited down the street in my car for her to come home, planning to introduce myself. I bumped into her as she was running down the steps. Someone broke into her place. Tell me it wasn't you."

"Shit! They beat us to it," Murray said.

"They're not dumb." Luke put the phone on speaker and set it on the kitchen island. He opened his refrigerator, pulled out a cold beer, and twisted off the bottle cap. He needed something to cool his nerves.

"We're counting on you, Corrado."

"I got it, Murray. Quit worrying."

Lots of lives were in the balance. Luke couldn't screw this up. He took a long pull on his beer.

"The Santisi woman is the key. Use your charms on her, Loverboy." Murray chuckled.

Luke sank onto one of the high stools arranged around the island. "If I ever find the person who gave me that nickname, he won't be long for this world."

"There's no doubt you're catnip to the ladies. Chill out. We've all got nicknames."

"Care to know yours?" Luke asked.

"No way."

"Then stuff the Loverboy shit. I'll do my job. Don't I always?" Luke disconnected the call as regret sucker-punched him in the gut. He always followed orders, except for that one time. And that time a woman died.

He wouldn't let that happen with Anita Santisi.

CHAPTER TWO

Anita locked her salon, turned her coat collar up against the brisk wind, and strode down the street. Darting her eyes to the two people about to pass her, she wished there were more pedestrians on the sidewalks in center city Philadelphia this Monday night. Since the break-in two days ago, she'd felt unsafe and vulnerable. And paranoid, sensing danger around every corner and from strangers she passed on the streets.

Because her salon and spa had been especially busy today, she'd closed later than usual and was the last one to leave. She could have asked one of her employees to stay but she didn't want to keep them from their families. As one of the top salons in the city, her clientele increased every week. She'd worked hard and her success made her happy. Yet, a part of her felt empty, as if something was missing. She pulled her coat tighter. She should be pleased with her life. She had everything she'd ever wanted. *But there's more*, a small voice inside whispered. Anita picked up her pace as if she could outrun her thoughts.

She felt a presence before she heard the heavy footsteps behind her. Anita slowed, and the footsteps slowed too. She walked faster and the other steps quickened. Willing herself to remain calm, she glanced across the street where a few others walked. She should cross over. There was safety in numbers. She caught her reflection in a shop window. The window also reflected the person following her, a large, bulky man.

Fear whipped through her. Holding her purse close, she jogged as fast as her high heels would allow. And bumped into a wall of pure muscle.

Strong hands gripped her upper arms. She inhaled the masculine scent of soap and outdoors.

"We've got to stop meeting like this." A smooth male voice, a familiar voice, spoke close to her ear.

Anita glanced up and met the chocolate eyes of Luke Corrado. Pushing away, she smoothed a gloved hand down her coat and shot a furtive look behind her. The bulky man had disappeared. Relief coursed through her.

She turned back to Luke. "I seem to have a habit of bumping into you. What are you doing here anyway?" She winced at her accusatory tone.

He held up his hands. "Hey, I'm walking around, getting acquainted with the city."

"I didn't mean to sound so, well, so snappish. Do you work around here?" After her break-in she had to be careful. Strange how Luke happened to be here tonight. And how he had happened to be at the bottom of her steps the other day. But he'd driven away the guy following her now. She smiled, trying to relax. It was mere coincidence that brought her and Luke together again.

He returned her smile, and her insides melted like frost on a sunny day. Damn that dimple of his!

"I'm consulting with a company a few blocks over on Walnut." He frowned. "You doing okay? I noticed them fixing your door and putting in a security system yesterday, and I saw you got a new sofa and chairs. Quick work, especially for a Sunday."

"My cousin Franco has good contacts." She tilted her head to look up at him. "Are you keeping an eye on me, Mr. Corrado?"

"Just being neighborly. And call me Luke."

A blast of icy air shot down the street, making her shiver.

Luke cupped her elbow. "Let's go somewhere warm. How about it? A drink between neighbors."

She looked into those eyes of his and found it hard to breathe. In a black overcoat, unbuttoned to reveal a white shirt and charcoal gray suit, he was too damn sexy for his own good— or hers. She didn't need any complications in her life and Luke

13

Corrado had danger written all over his striking face.

Yet, those eyes. That dimple. What the hell! "Sure, I'd love to have a drink with you."

◇◇◇

They found a small table in an upscale bistro on Chestnut Street. After ordering their drinks, Anita excused herself to go to the ladies' room.

Luke sat facing the door in case the creep who'd been following Anita made an appearance. He'd watched the guy stalk her, then quickly disappear when Luke showed up. Apparently, the goons who'd ransacked her house hadn't found what they'd been looking for. That could be bad news for her. The international criminal organization wouldn't stop until they got what they wanted.

His gaze focused on Anita as she walked slowly back to the table. His groin tightened as he watched her move with lithe, animal grace. Slim and petite, with long black, silky hair that streamed down her back, dressed all in black—from her high-heeled boots, slacks and sweater, to her leather jacket—she was a sexy kitten he'd like to make purr. He wanted to bring out her wild side, too, wanted to see her claws.

Whoa, guy. You've been down that road before and look what happened. His job was to protect Anita Santisi and find that list before the cartel found it. Being wildly attracted to the woman he'd sworn to protect wasn't part of the job.

He stood when she reached their table. She raised one perfect black eyebrow and sat. "I didn't think men stood for women anymore."

"This one does. My mama taught me right." His mama, the single parent who'd worked herself to death to make sure he got an education so he didn't join one of the gangs around Tucson. Luke's sister hadn't been so lucky. He pushed back the bad memories. He had enough of those to last a lifetime.

Their drinks came, and he held up his glass of red wine in salute. "To my neighbor."

They clinked glasses and she sipped her wine, watching

him over the rim. Setting down her glass, she met his gaze. "You said you were working with a company on Walnut. What type work do you do?"

I lie for a living.

"I'm a consultant," he said instead. "I founded a software company and recently sold it. I couldn't handle all my new leisure time, so I hire myself out to consult for other firms. My work takes me all over the country and the world." The lies, the cover the Agency had come up with, rolled easily off his tongue. The longer he was in this spirit-destroying job, the easier the lies became. He feared he'd one day lose the real Luke Corrado, the barrio kid with dreams of making the world a better place. He'd seen enough of the underbelly of life to shatter those dreams. At least for this mission, the Agency had allowed him to use his real name and background.

"A software consultant," Anita said. "Impressive."

He shrugged. "What do you do?" But he knew, and had been in the vicinity of her salon tonight planning to *accidently* bump into her. The Agency had thoroughly investigated her, had determined she probably had nothing to do with Sweeney's disappearance, and was a pawn in this dangerous game.

"I run a salon and spa farther down on Chestnut," she said.

"Now *that's* impressive." He smiled and saw how her eyes, her golden-brown sexy eyes, lit up. His smile had that effect on women and he had used it to his advantage many times in his line of work, each time crumbling another piece of his soul.

"My salon is one of the top ones in Philly," she said with a note of pride.

He raised his glass. "Even more impressive." He glanced at her ring finger. "No husband or ex-husband or boyfriend lurking in the background?"

She blinked, and sadness flitted across her face for the span of a heartbeat. Then she shot him a beautiful smile. He'd be willing to bet her smile had broken a few male hearts. His gaze locked on her lips, those full, pink lips that seemed to beg for his kisses. He shifted uncomfortably.

15

"No husband," she said. "Past or current." She stared down at the tiled table, then back up to him. "I don't need a husband. Never did."

"Boyfriend?" Their investigation revealed no man in her life after Sweeney, but he wanted to be sure. And a small part of him, the personal part he kept hidden, wanted to verify she had no one.

"No boyfriend either," she said and shrugged.

"What's wrong with the men in this town? A beautiful woman like you, unattached."

She rolled her eyes. "Why does everyone think I need a man? Maybe I don't want to be attached."

<><><>

An hour and a half later, Anita and Luke climbed the steps to their adjoining condos. When they'd left the bistro, he'd insisted on walking her to her car. As they'd strolled down the street to her parking garage, Luke seemed on edge, looking around, as if he expected something to happen.

They rode in her car to the lot where he'd parked his, and he'd followed her home, his Lexus staying close behind her Mercedes. While she admired his old-fashioned chivalry, a feeling, an instinct, told her more than good manners was behind it. When they got to her door, she shrugged off the feeling and turned to him. "Thanks for the drink, neighbor."

He stepped closer until they were a whisper apart. "You're welcome, *neighbor*. Let's do it again."

At his nearness and the huskiness in his voice, her heart raced. She should move away. She didn't want to.

He cupped her shoulders and bent his head. She lifted hers.

His lips took hers in a gentle kiss. She pressed closer and returned his kiss, opening her mouth in invitation. His tongue joined hers. He tasted like wine and mint. A small groan escaped her. She dropped her purse and keys and wound her arms around his neck.

Anita gave in to her feelings. She was in heaven. Luke kissed like an angel, or maybe a devil. She wanted more, so much more.

A door slammed down the street, dropping her back to Earth. She pushed away from Luke. She should so not have let him kiss her. But, wow, what a kiss! Her breathing ragged, she stared at him.

"I've wanted to do that from the first minute I saw you," he whispered.

She picked up her purse and keys and jammed her door key into her lock. "Just because I live next door doesn't mean you can take advantage of me." She tempered her warning with a smile.

He gave her a wicked grin in return. "I wouldn't think of taking advantage of you."

No way did she believe that. "Thanks again for the drink. Good night."

"Make sure to set your security system." Luke watched her slip inside.

Anita disengaged her alarm, reset it, and leaned against the closed door. Damn! The man could kiss. She wondered what else he could do.

"Easy, girl, you're off men for now. Remember? God knows where John Sweeney is. He dumped you. You are so not ready to start up with another guy."

Determined to keep Luke at arm's length, she hurried up the steps to her bedroom and her lonely bed.

◇◇◇

Luke entered his condo and headed into his living area, opulently furnished by the owner. The entire loft looked like this—overstuffed sectional and matching chairs in browns and golds, pillows, heavy walnut furniture. Sure wasn't his taste. He preferred sparse, minimal, modern. What did it matter? He was rarely in one place for long and kept a barely furnished apartment in Tucson. Lucky for him and the Agency they were able to rent this place. Someone else had put a down payment on it, but the Agency, through careful manipulation, managed to secure it instead. Pulling off his jacket, Luke threw it onto a chair and headed to the small bar tucked into a corner.

He filled a snifter with a splash of brandy, his thoughts on Anita. Damn, she could kiss. She'd had him hot and bothered from the first time he'd seen her. If she could kiss like that, how would it be to make love to her? He couldn't go there. His job was to gain her trust, not sleep with her.

CHAPTER THREE

Loud ringing jerked Luke from a deep sleep. Instantly alert, he grabbed his secure cell phone from the night table. Raking a hand over his hair, he hit the talk button and glanced at the clock. Only trouble called at three in the morning.

"Yeah? What's up?" he asked.

"I just got a call from my source at police headquarters. A body was found floating in the Delaware," Murray said. "My source says it appears to be Sweeney, although there's not much to go by after two months in the water."

"Shit!"

"The ME did a cursory exam. Sweeney had been tortured and shot execution style." Murray hesitated. "He went through hell."

"He didn't deserve that. No one does." Luke jumped up from the bed and began pacing. "Sons of bitches. We've got to get those scumbags."

"We will. Thanks to Sweeney's work we know the crime syndicate's leader is here in Philadelphia. We'll get him." Murray cleared his throat. "Too bad Sweeney didn't get the name to us before he...he died. He was a real hero, but no one will know."

"When this is over, I want to visit John's parents. The Kupinski's need to know their son died a hero."

"We can arrange that," Murray said.

Anger boiled in Luke, a flaming cauldron that wouldn't be extinguished until they got the scum responsible for Sweeney's death. And the death and enslavement of so many innocents. But now, they had to concentrate on the mission, to ensure Sweeney didn't die in vain.

"When Sweeney went silent, I alerted my contact at police headquarters to be on the lookout for a body." Murray sighed. "We should have seen this coming."

"Sweeney wouldn't have dropped his cover," Luke said. "You going to ID him?"

"I'm going down there later this morning."

Special Agent John Sweeney, real name John Kupinski, working deep undercover, had managed to infiltrate the international crime organization and had been working on learning the leader's identity. Before he disappeared, he'd phoned his Agency contact to say he was close to finding the leader's name. He'd mentioned he'd heard about a list that in the crime syndicate's possession would be deadly to the Agency and to international groups investigating the criminal cartel. Sweeney had been sure he could get the list and hand it off to the Agency before the gang delivered it to their leader. They never heard from him again.

Murray was still talking. Luke refocused.

"...and my source at police headquarters will smooth things over, make sure the cops treat Sweeney's murder as a botched mugging."

"Damn it," Luke said. "How many more have to die, or worse, before we bring down the bastards who did this?" Too wound up to sleep, he held the phone to his ear and headed to his kitchen. It would be a long night. He had to think, to strategize. He'd string up the leader himself if he ever got his hands on him. The Agency and the law be damned.

"How's it going with the Santisi woman?" Murray asked.

"I'm getting to know her. Had some drinks with her last night." And kissed those full, sexy lips of hers. But Murray didn't need to know that.

"Good, but move it on. Gain her confidence. It's looking more and more like Sweeney gave the list to her. For God's sake, don't let her know anything's up. If she panics and the syndicate finds out we know about the list, all hell breaks loose."

"Yeah, yeah. I know the stakes and I know how to do my

job."

"If we didn't think you could do the job, we wouldn't have brought you here. You only screwed up that one time. You let your personal feelings get in the way. You won't do it again."

"Gotta go." Luke disconnected the call. He didn't want to talk about Mexico, but it haunted his dreams, even his waking moments.

Anita worked on her client's hair, her mind on Luke. Since that kiss three days ago, her thoughts constantly drifted to him. She wanted to kiss him again, to do more than kiss. Her insides heated thinking of him, of his touch, his scent, his gentleness edged with passion. Much as she hated to admit it, his protectiveness toward her had broken off a chunk of the wall she'd so carefully constructed around her heart.

"Anita, there are two detectives here for you." Molly, her receptionist, stood behind her, interrupting her thoughts.

"Detectives?" Anita turned off the blow dryer and met Molly's frightened eyes in the mirror. "It's okay. Offer them some coffee or tea. I'll be right there."

Molly swallowed. "Will do."

When she'd gone, Anita turned back to her client, a very young trophy wife of an elderly billionaire. "Do you mind if Darlene finishes you, Tiffany?"

"No problem," Tiffany said. "Maybe they found out who broke into your house."

"That has to be why they're here." Of course it was.

After calling Darlene over to finish for her, Anita headed to the reception area. Two uncomfortable-looking middle-aged men in crumpled, badly-fitting suits sat in the delicate chairs.

When she approached, they stood and flashed Philadelphia police badges.

"I'm Anita Santisi, the owner. Did you find the people who broke into my house last week?"

"No, Ms. Santisi, that's not why we're here," one of them said.

A chill ran up her spine.

"Is there someplace we can talk in private?" the other asked.

"My office." She gestured to a closed door on one side of the reception area. "We can talk there."

Anita slipped into her office, the men following. She shut the door and leaned against it. Fighting her anxiety, she folded her arms across her chest and faced the men.

"I'm Prescott, and this is Duffy," the first guy who'd spoken said.

Anita nodded. "What's this about?"

Prescott took a notebook from his jacket pocket and flipped pages. Notebook in hand he studied her. Her anxiety ratcheted to dread.

"We understand you know a man named John Sweeney, owns an antique shop at Second and Arch," he said. "When we interviewed his employees, your name came up."

She tensed, drew in a breath, gulped air. "Yes. I dated John for about six months, but I haven't seen him in over two months. Has something happened to him?"

"I'm afraid so, Ms. Santisi," Duffy said. "We found his body in the Delaware the other day."

She gasped and put a hand to her mouth. "How?" she finally managed.

"Murdered," Prescott said. "Probably a mugging gone bad. But we have to investigate all possibilities."

"Murdered? John? He was an antiques dealer, for God's sake. Who would kill him?" She was rambling. *John, dead?* Her mind refused to accept that. "This has to be a mistake. Are you sure it was him?"

Duffy nodded. "One of his acquaintances ID'd him."

Afraid her legs wouldn't hold her, Anita walked to the desk and sat on the edge.

"As part of the investigation, we need to ask you some questions," Duffy said.

For the next half hour, the cops grilled her, asking the same questions over and over. Did she know of any enemies John had? Was he into anything illegal? Did he carry a lot of cash with him?

Did she know why anyone would want to kill him? Over and over until Anita wanted to scream for them to leave her alone to deal with her grief.

Finally, they left. Hugging herself, Anita stood in the middle of her office, too frozen by shock to move.

A few minutes later, there was a knock at her door. It opened a crack, and Justin, her top stylist, peeked in. "Are you okay? Elaine Cutford has been waiting a while."

Anita smoothed a hand over her hair. "I'll be out in a minute." With effort, she forced her features into a composed mask. She didn't know if she could deal with Elaine's constant prattling about fashion, parties, and the latest juicy stories of the city's power elite.

Justin left, but didn't close the door. Anita heard the tap of high heels on the wood floor. A minute later, Elaine Cutford, in black skinny jeans, sky-high silver heels, and a tight red sweater that showed off her impressive new breasts, entered the office.

"Anita, what's happened? Molly said those two guys who just left are detectives. Is there a problem?" Elaine grabbed Anita's hands and held them between her own, studying Anita with heavily made-up green eyes. Elaine, fifty and stylish, with long red-blonde hair, full collagen-injected lips and high cheekbones thanks to the city's most expensive cosmetic surgeon, was Anita's best client.

Elaine and her husband Mace were heavily into real estate and owned several high-rise buildings in Philadelphia. One of the richest and most influential couples in the city, they'd loaned Anita money to start her salon after Kent, her rat bastard of an ex-boyfriend, had cleaned out her bank account. Elaine sent wealthy clients to the salon, too. Anita owed the Cutfords, big time. Feeling guilty about her unkind thoughts earlier, Anita tried to smile.

But instead of a smile, the tears she'd been holding flowed freely. "Oh, Elaine, John Sweeney is dead. Murdered."

Elaine stepped back. "John? That nice man you dated?"

Anita could only nod. Elaine held out her arms and Anita

fell into them.

Finally, Anita pushed free and swiped the tears from her face. "Thanks, Elaine. I haven't seen John in over two months. He said he was going on a business trip, and he never came back."

Anita put a fist to her mouth, fighting for composure. "I stopped at his shop when I didn't hear from him, and his employees said he'd texted them that he'd sold the shop and to close it up. And he'd be back soon. I figured he'd dumped me." She blinked away tears. "He's dead."

"How terrible. Did the police say how he was murdered?"

"Just that he was pulled out of the Delaware." She shivered. "That poor man."

"Do they have any leads?"

Anita frowned. Elaine was beginning to sound like one of the cops. "If they do, they wouldn't tell me."

"Of course they wouldn't. I don't understand what they could want with you."

"They had some questions for me. But I wasn't much help."

Elaine grabbed one of Anita's hands. "I'm so sorry, darling."

Anita forced a smile. "Let's work on your hair."

Elaine returned her smile. "After all you've been through lately, you need to get away for awhile. Why don't you use our place in Atlantic City for a few days?"

"I can't do that, Elaine. It wouldn't be right. The salon's really busy. And John's dead."

"Justin can run things for you here. You can't bring John back, darling, and you need to take care of yourself."

"I'll think about it."

"Take someone with you, a girlfriend." Elaine's full lips tilted in a wicked grin. "Or a man."

Getting away from Philadelphia with its break-ins and murders sounded like a good idea. Maybe she'd take Elaine up on her offer.

And maybe she'd ask Luke to go with her. She hadn't seen him since that amazing kiss.

He'd be good company in Atlantic City. But as a friend only. Of course.

CHAPTER FOUR

That evening, Anita sipped her wine, the TV muted. The local news had just reported the body pulled from the Delaware several days ago was positively identified as John Sweeney, owner of an antique store in the city.

John, with his laughing blue eyes, had always been good to her. The last time she'd seen him, he'd told her he loved her. He'd sounded almost desperate, but she hadn't been able to return the sentiment. She'd liked John, enjoyed his company. But love?

Not for her, not again.

Anita fought tears. She rarely cried, but the break-in and now John's death left her feeling defenseless. Profound sadness swirled through her. She kept imagining them pulling John from the Delaware. John. Her friend. Gone. A single tear slipped down her cheek and she swiped it away. She'd rather that he'd dumped her. Fighting nausea, she set down her wine and wrapped her arms around her midriff.

The doorbell rang. She jumped. For a half second when she'd gotten home, she'd been tempted to call Jo to come over and keep her company, but Jo was pregnant, and Anita didn't want to put any stress on her. Besides, Anita had had no one to depend on but herself for many years and she could handle her own problems.

Pushing up from the sofa, she headed toward the door, prepared to send away whoever it was. When she looked through the peephole and saw Luke, her heart lurched. The feel of his lips when he'd kissed her flashed into her mind, sending a heat wave through her.

She opened the door. "Luke, what are you doing here?"

"By how quickly you opened that door, I can tell you didn't set your security alarm when you got home."

"Why set it when I'm here?"

"You have to be careful. Promise you'll set it at all times."

She frowned. "I promise. Did you come here to tell me that?"

He grinned, showing his dimple, and a little of her grief melted with his smile.

"I saw you come home," he said, "and I figured maybe you hadn't eaten yet. I'll take you to dinner if you don't have any plans."

"Thanks for the offer, but I don't feel like eating."

Narrowing his eyes, he studied her. "What's wrong? Have you been crying?"

"Crying? I never cry."

"May I come in?"

"I'm not very good company."

"Why don't you let me be the judge of that? I'll cook you dinner."

"I'm not hungry."

"When you smell my cooking, you will be," he said, smiling.

Her mind said to send him away, but his kindness brought a lump to her throat. And she didn't want to be alone.

She stood back to let him enter.

◇◇◇

"I never knew tuna casserole could be that good." With a contented sigh, Anita leaned back in her chair. The dining room table bore the remnants of the dinner Luke had cooked. She picked up her glass and sipped the crisp, cold white wine.

He saluted her with his wine goblet. "Glad you liked my dinner. If you'd had any Mexican ingredients I could have really amazed you with my culinary skills." He laughed. "Maybe amazed isn't the right word, but I'm pretty good with Mexican dishes."

"I can't believe you were able to put that delicious casserole together with what you found in my pantry and refrigerator."

"It was a challenge. I take it you're not a cook."

She shrugged. "Why cook when there are takeout and restaurants?"

He chuckled. "Why indeed." His features grew serious and he leaned closer across the table. "Ready to talk about what has you so upset? I'm a good listener."

She glanced down and studied her wine, wishing it could tell her the meaning of all that had happened lately. Realizing she hadn't hidden her sadness, she raised her gaze to Luke's.

"I learned today that a dear friend died." She braced herself. "He was murdered."

Luke put his hand over hers. "I'm sorry. That's tough."

"John was a really nice guy. We dated for six months. About eight weeks ago he disappeared. He frequently went out of town on buying trips for his antique shop, but he always called me while he was on the road. I called and texted him a few times, and when I didn't hear from him, I figured he'd lost interest in me."

She pulled her hand from Luke's and sipped more wine. "My track record with men isn't good." She didn't want to tell Luke she was usually the one who ran from commitment.

"Did you love him?" Luke asked quietly.

"As a friend. He wanted to take our relationship deeper, but I couldn't."

Luke studied her with an intensity that made her gulp the rest of her wine.

"He dealt in antiques?" he asked.

Surprised at his question, she nodded.

He looked around the room. "Are any of his antiques here?"

"Why do you ask?"

"I'm interested in them. I plan to start buying some if I ever settle down in one place."

Quirking an eyebrow, she scanned him. "You don't look like a guy who collects antiques."

27

He laughed. "What kind of guy do I look like?"

Like someone who'd be terrific in bed.

Instead she said, "John gave me a few pieces as gifts."

"I'd like to see them sometime."

"Oookay."

Something he'd said earlier pushed forward in her mind and she caught his gaze. "You said you plan to settle down one of these days. I thought you liked traveling for your consulting business, that staying in one place is boring."

"I do like to keep on the move, but it's starting to get old. I sold my house in California, but I'd like to buy another one there." He picked up his own wine and took a sip, set down the glass. "I've rented the place next to yours for two months."

She'd known about the rental, but now that she'd gotten to know Luke better, the thought of his leaving sent a surprising jolt of sadness through her.

Once the kitchen was clean, they sat in the living room eating ice cream. Feeling relaxed for the first time since she'd heard about John, Anita curled up on the end of the sofa with her legs tucked under her. She studied Luke's profile. His strong hawk-like nose, high cheekbones, and bronzed skin hinted at American Indian heritage. Her fingers itched to touch his smooth skin to see if it was as firm as it looked.

He caught her staring. Something pulsed between them, something hot and wicked. His sexy eyes intoxicated her more than the wine they'd had at dinner.

Forcing her gaze away, she stared at the fire in the fireplace. The flames from the gas fire licked their way toward the chimney and freedom. Anita wanted freedom, too, from the heartache of John's death, from the constant fear she'd been under since the break-in.

"A penny for them," Luke said, drawing her attention.

"My thoughts aren't worth that." Setting her empty ice cream bowl on the coffee table, she faced him again. "Tell me about you."

"Not much to tell. Raised in Tucson. My dad took off right

after my sister Sofia was born. My mom worked as a maid for several wealthy families." Luke's lips tilted in a soft smile. "We lived in the barrio. It was a hard life, but my mom did the best she could."

Anita smiled. "Your mom must be proud of you."

Sadness flitted over his features. "She's gone now, but she lived to see me graduate from college. I was the first in my family to go."

"What about your sister?"

A haunted look came into his eyes. "She died when she was eighteen."

"I'm sorry."

"It was a long time ago." He stood. "I'd better get going."

Luke had closed down.

She stood too. "Thanks again for dinner," she said, sorry to lose the camaraderie they'd shared. When they got to the door, she reached for the handle.

Luke put his hand over hers, stopping her from opening it. "Anita," he whispered. His eyes lit with desire that sparked a response low in her belly.

Then she was in his arms. His mouth, soft, yet firm, took hers in a scorching kiss that turned the heat within her to a flaming, needy fire.

His tongue demanded entry. She parted her lips, inviting his possession. His tongue stroked, pulling her deeper under his sensual spell. He tasted of coffee, chocolate ice cream, and man. She felt his erection, hard and hot against her stomach, as she inhaled his outdoor scent tinged with the musk of his arousal.

He buried his hands in her hair and backed her against the door, settling his hard-muscled body between her legs. His mouth left her lips to nibble on her earlobe and trail a path down her neck to the curve of her shoulder.

"Luke." Her whispered word floated between them.

He suddenly pulled away, leaving her feeling torn, bereft. With a small cry, she reached for him.

He took both her hands in his. "Anita, I'm sorry. I didn't

mean for that to happen. You're grieving and I took advantage of you. Forgive me." He smiled. "And set your security alarm when I leave."

Then, like an intruder in the night, he slipped out the door. Hand to her mouth, she leaned against the closed door. She'd wanted Luke, needed him to take away her pain and fill the lonely places in her heart and soul.

But he was gone.

CHAPTER FIVE

Much later, when Luke went to bed, hoping for some much-needed rest, he tossed and turned for hours, his mind churning with his need for Anita, the mission, Sweeney's death, the futility of it all. Finally, close to dawn, he fell into an exhausted sleep.

The thug punched him in the face again. The sound of bones crunching told Luke they'd broken his nose. He spit out blood and pulled at the zip ties holding him. The ties wouldn't budge. The men who had him knew what they were doing.

"If you want to live, Señor Correa, you'd better start talking. Who do you work for?"

"I work for Mendoza," Luke said through the pain. "You know that."

"We got info you're working for the Feds."

"Someone's playing you. You guys know me. Do I look like I work for the Feds?" He forced out the words and tried to ignore the metallic taste of blood in his mouth. The Mexicans knew him as Luis Correa. If they were still calling him by his undercover name, his true identity was safe.

Pedro, the largest and the meanest of the group, approached him. Pedro had stood in the shadows while his men worked Luke over. Pedro was a sadist, and the way he clenched and unclenched his fists told Luke the worst was yet to come. He prepared for death.

"Mendoza hears you been fucking his sister," Pedro said. "He don't take kindly to men screwing with Maria."

"I've never touched Maria," Luke lied. "I love her and want to marry her." He didn't need to lie about that.

"Mendoza will kill Maria before he allows her to marry a Federale."

A wicked glint in his small, dark eyes, Pedro raised his fist. "After I get through with you, your face won't be so pretty." With another wicked laugh, he said, "And that other part of you the ladies like so much won't be so pretty either."

Luke jerked awake, heart hammering. The nightmares had started again. It had been almost three years since that horrendous night Luke was forced to flee Mexico without Maria. Luke had been close to finding the evidence that would have put Mendoza in prison for the rest of his days. But the drug cartel leader had escaped the Feds again that time. His far-flung crime network still protected him.

Special agents and Mexican police had raided the cabin where Luke was being tortured, arresting Mendoza's men. They'd saved Luke's life, and to protect his cover, they let the cartel think they were sending him to a separate prison after his wounds were tended to. Later, the Agency put out word that Luke had been killed in prison. But Mendoza hadn't believed Luke was dead. The cartel leader put a high bounty on Luke's head. The Agency had ordered Luke to stay out of Mexico. But he'd disobeyed orders and gone back that one last time, for Maria.

Murray had intervened, and the bureau had only given Luke a reprimand and sent him to a therapist who tried to help him through his guilt. Nothing would take away the guilt that he hadn't protected Maria as he hadn't protected his sister Sofia. Both dead.

Luke glanced at the bedside clock. Four a.m. Pulling himself up, he leaned against the headboard. The room was chilly, but he welcomed the discomfort, using the cold as penance for his sins. He'd learned to live with the guilt but it still ate at his gut.

He closed his eyes, letting the painful memories wash over him. After a time, his thoughts strayed to Anita. He'd kissed her again. He had no right, but she tempted him as no other woman ever had, not even Maria. Anita's compelling combination of hard-edged sophistication tempered with her vulnerability spoke to his protective instincts. A lot of good those instincts were when he hadn't been able to save the two women he'd loved.

What had happened with Maria couldn't happen again with another woman. Yet, the sadness in Anita's large golden-brown eyes touched the lonely places in his heart.

◇◇◇

Anita leaned against the door in the ladies' room at her salon, catching a few minutes alone. They'd been busy all morning. That was a good thing, not only for the success of her business but because it kept her from obsessing over Luke and their kiss last night.

Guilt shot through her. John was dead, and she was lusting after another man. She'd been fond of John, but their affair hadn't been about love. Love led to happiness followed by despair. She didn't deserve happiness, and she'd had enough despair to last her lifetime. She'd loved her father and he was taken from her when she'd needed him the most. Then Kent. Men didn't stay around—a hard lesson she'd learned well.

Yet—Luke had come into her life. No man had ever thrilled her the way Luke did. But, it was more than that. She recognized strength in Luke. She instinctively knew he was someone she could depend on. But she didn't need a man or anyone to protect her. She'd been on her own for too long.

Her cell phone rang. Glad to be yanked from her disturbing thoughts, she pulled her phone from her pants pocket and checked the ID. Elaine Cutford. Sometimes Anita wondered if she'd made a pact with the devil when she accepted the loan from the Cutfords. She'd paid them back years ago, but they still acted as if she was at their beck and call. True, they'd been good to her, but she didn't like being jerked around. And the Cutfords were masters at manipulating people to get what they wanted. If she pulled back from them, they'd make sure their friends stopped coming to her salon. Yes, she'd made a pact with the devil.

Putting a smile on her face, hoping it would show in her voice, she answered the call. "Hello, Elaine. I didn't see you in today's appointment book. Do you have a hair emergency? You know I'm here to help."

"Darling, I'm fine. My hair is perfect, thanks to your skilled hands." Elaine practically purred.

Anita's sensors went on alert. Elaine wanted something.

"Mace and I need a little favor, please, darling."

"Of course, what can I do for you?" Anita made a face at her reflection in the mirror. She always felt a little dirty when dealing with the Cutfords, especially Mace.

"You know that intimate Christmas party Mace and I plan at our Rittenhouse Square penthouse?"

"Of course. And I look forward to it."

"There's a little problem. We had a small fire. Nothing serious, but our electrical wiring is cooked. The electrician says it can't be fixed in time for the party."

"I'm sorry, Elaine. Will you move the party to your Main Line house?"

"Darling, that house is too big for the intimate gathering we want. We know this is a lot to ask of you, but could we use your loft?"

"My loft?" Shock propelled Anita away from the door. The Cutfords could afford to buy a new penthouse just for their party. Why would they want her little place? "Seriously, Elaine, my place isn't what you or your guests are used to."

"It's a sweet place, just right. I'll have my decorator call you later to make arrangements to come out and get it in the Christmas spirit. My caterer and wait staff will handle everything. I'll even send my cleaning crew over before and after the party. You can keep all the decorations. It's a win-win for everyone."

But not for me. "I'm not sure I'm in the mood to entertain. Not after John's death."

"Anita, dear, this will help you get over your grief. And Mace and I will do the entertaining. You just have to be your beautiful self. Gotta go."

◇◇◇

Driving home from work later that day, Anita had the uneasy feeling of being followed. When she looked in the rearview mirror, everything looked normal. The car that had been following her for blocks held a family. The recent happenings were making her paranoid. And now she felt trapped, too, into hosting a party for the Cutfords.

She parked in her spot in front of the condo and exited her car. As she turned to lock it, someone grabbed her from behind, and a large, cold, calloused hand pressed against her mouth. She inhaled the odor of tobacco.

"Listen, girly, you have something we want. You know what it is. Give it to us and we'll go easy on you. But right now, we're gonna take you for a little ride to convince you to play nice."

Hot, burning fear clogged her lungs, but a sudden surge of adrenaline shot through her, giving her strength. She bit his finger and struggled to get away.

With his hand still on her mouth and his other arm around her waist, the man swore, locked her against him, and began dragging her to a car parked in the middle of the street with the engine running.

She poked him in the ribs with her elbow. He grunted but didn't loosen his hold. If they got her in that car, she'd never come out alive.

The slap of running feet echoed along the quiet street. The man holding her twisted around, released her, and shoved her away from him. She fell sprawling onto the ground. Her attacker jumped into the waiting car. With a squeal of tires, it sped away.

"Anita, darlin'," a familiar voice said. Harris, Jo's partner in their security company, reached down to help her up.

She brushed dirt from her pants with shaking hands and winced. The heels of her hands were scratched and raw, and the knees of her pants were torn. She pushed hair back from her face before looking up at Harris.

"Thanks, Harris," she said in a thin voice. "I was so scared he was going to force me into that car." She'd been riding on sheer nerves during the attack, fighting to stay alive. Now that it was over, her insides trembled and her legs turned to mush. She swayed and began to fall.

Harris grabbed her, gripping her upper arms. "It's okay. You're okay."

"I'll be all right. Just shaken up." When he released her, she frowned. "What are you doing here?"

"I'm sorry," he said. "I should have been faster. I'm on your security detail tonight. I followed you home, but just when you got out of your car, bright headlights coming the other way distracted me. When I looked up, that goon had you. Let's get you into your place in case they come back. Then we'll call the police."

He bent to retrieve the keys and purse she'd dropped and took her elbow.

She pulled back. "What do you mean, you're on my security detail?"

"Jo and Franco didn't tell you?"

"No."

"Keepin' an eye on you like they asked."

"They should have run it by me first." She closed her eyes for a second, composing herself. Meeting Harris's gaze, she said, "Still, I'm happy you were here tonight. Thanks."

He grinned and took her elbow again, leading her to the steps. "And what would you have said if they'd asked?"

"I would have told them no, but now I'm glad they didn't ask first. They worry too much though."

"They can't help worryin'. You're family. I or one of my men will watch over you every day while you're at work and follow you home every night. You won't even know we're there. As long as you set your security system at home and don't answer the door to strangers, you should be all right there."

He handed her purse to her but held onto her keys. When they reached her door, he twisted her key into the lock.

"I want my nice, boring life back," she said.

"It'll work out. We'll keep you safe and you'll get your life back." He gestured for her to move. "Let's go in."

They entered the loft and she disengaged her alarm. Once she'd reset it, she and Harris went into the living room.

"Sit. Relax," Harris said. "I need to call the police."

The doorbell rang. Harris stiffened and pulled out his gun. He walked quickly to the door and looked through the peephole. Turning to her with a frown, he nodded for her to look.

She peeked out to see Luke staring back at her. "It's my neighbor."

"He okay?"

"Yes."

"Let him in."

When she opened the door, Luke smiled and entered. She shut the door after him. "I saw your car and…" He noticed Harris still holding his gun. Luke's smile faded. His body tensed, as if readying for a fight. "What's going on?"

"It's okay, Luke. This is Harris. Apparently my bodyguard. And, Harris, this is Luke Corrado."

"Bodyguard?" Luke said.

Harris put away his gun and held out his hand to shake Luke's. "I own a security firm with Anita's cousin Jo. Jo and Franco thought it would be a good idea to have security on Anita. Good thing too. Someone accosted her tonight."

"What?" Luke reached for Anita and grabbed her hands, holding her at arms' length. "Are you okay?"

Luke's concern brought her fear back to the surface. She bit down on her lip to stop its trembling and struggled to keep her voice level. "Something happened." She swallowed. "Thanks to Harris, I'm not hurt."

Luke didn't look at Harris, but focused his attention on Anita. Worry etched on his face, he tugged on her hands. "Sit down and I'll get you a glass of wine."

"I'm okay. Really."

"You need to take it easy," Luke insisted.

"Listen to the man, darlin'. Try to relax. I'll call the police." Harris pulled his cell phone from his pocket.

Luke frowned at him before he led Anita to the sofa.

"Ready to tell me what happened?" Luke asked a short while later as he sat next to her on the sofa while they waited for the police. Anita and Luke were drinking wine, and Harris sat across from them, drinking from a bottle of water.

Anita raised her gaze to Luke's. "Some guy grabbed me as I was locking my car. He tried to drag me into another car. He said they were going to take me for a ride to convince me to give them what they want. Thankfully, Harris was on security detail and chased the guy away."

A muscle worked in Luke's jaw and he turned to Harris. "Some security detail you are. You should never have let that scum get close to her."

Anita set her glass onto the table and touched Luke's arm. "It's all right, Luke. I wasn't hurt, and Harris was there."

"Corrado's right," Harris said. "I fell down on the job. It won't happen again, darlin'."

"See that it doesn't." Anger vibrated from Luke's voice. He set down his own glass and looked at Harris. "Let's walk over there where we can talk in private." He nodded toward the opposite side of the large room.

◇◇◇

Narrowing his eyes at the older man, Luke followed him. The guy's tall, muscular frame and short, graying hair shouted military, maybe Special Ops. For a big guy, Harris walked softly, but that softness could be deceptive.

The two men faced each other far enough away that Anita couldn't hear.

"What branch of the military were you in?" Luke asked, his voice low.

"Navy. I was a SEAL," Harris answered.

"I figured as much," Luke said. "Look, man, I didn't mean to ream you out in front of the lady, but you should be taking better care of her."

Harris's lips thinned and he studied Luke, as if trying to take his measure. "I may have fallen down tonight but thankfully she's okay. Don't worry. I won't let anything happen to her."

"See that you don't."

Harris stepped closer. "Whatever is between you and Anita is your business, but she's family. The whole Callahan-Tanner-Santisi clan is family to me. You mess with her or hurt her in any way and you'll have all of us on your ass."

"I care about Anita. Back off." Yet, Luke would have to leave when the mission was over. He didn't want to hurt Anita, and he wondered if he would.

"Damn." Luke ran a hand over his hair. "I know you're trying to protect her, but I'm worried about her. This attack tonight takes things to another level."

"We're on it." Harris frowned. "In what branch of the military did you serve?"

"I wasn't in the military."

"Be straight with me, Corrado. Who the hell are you? I understand why you're interested in Anita. She's a beautiful woman. But there's something else going down here. There are too many coincidences. You were close when her place was broken into. You seem to be always around when something happens."

"What are you implying?"

Harris held up his hands, palms raised. "Not implying anything, but I'm gettin' vibes about you. I can read people, and you're into something. I can feel it."

Luke wanted to bring Harris into his confidence, but he couldn't. He couldn't trust the ex-SEAL not to tell Anita and her family about Sweeney and the FBI. The Agency had to play their cards close. If the crime syndicate got even a whiff that the Agency knew about the list, years of careful undercover work would go up in smoke. Everyone, including Anita, had to remain in the dark.

"Look, man," Luke said. "I'm just a guy who started a software company and sold it for a lot of money. I'm a red-blooded male who's attracted to Anita. She's a terrific woman and I want to keep her safe. There's nothing more going on."

"I'll go along with that, Corrado, but I've got my eye on you."

CHAPTER SIX

Anita stood by the window and watched Harris climb into his car. Her nerves were in tatters even though he'd promised he'd be on her security detail for the next few days, rather than one of his men. The police had already gone after taking her statement.

Luke came up behind her and slipped his arms around her. She leaned into him. "Luke, I'm afraid. Nothing like this has ever happened to me before. I lead a quiet life, I go to dinner with friends, I take vacations. I don't hurt anyone. Why does someone want to hurt me?"

He pulled her closer. The steady beat of his heart vibrated against her back and calmed her.

"Are you sure you don't know what it is you have that these people want?"

She turned in his embrace. "Of course, I'm sure. I don't hang out with criminals." Needing to think clearly without his disturbing closeness, she reluctantly pulled free and crossed the room to sink onto the sofa. He followed and sat next to her.

"I don't understand what's happening, Luke. Not too long ago some people were trying to kill Franco. Jo was his bodyguard. Franco led a colorful life and knew some unsavory characters. But that's not me."

◇◇◇

Wanting to touch her, to comfort her, Luke took her hand in his and rubbed his fingers over her soft skin. "Has anyone lived here with you? Another guy?"

She shook her head. "No other guy has lived with me here."

"And what's with Harris? Did you two have a thing before?"

He didn't understand why he'd asked that, but he had to know.

She pulled back and looked at him as if he were a Christmas elf who'd suddenly materialized in front of her. "Harris? What makes you think that?"

"He calls you darlin' and you two are close."

Anita threw back her head and laughed. At least he'd made her laugh and forget her troubles for a few minutes. Finally, she looked at him grinning. "Harris calls all women darlin'. What is with you men? Franco confessed to Jo he was jealous of Harris at first and thought he and Jo'd had an affair. Now you. Harris is in his fifties, not that that's old, and he's a good-looking guy, but he's a little too old for Jo and me. He's become part of our family."

Luke glanced away. He was coming off like some jealous kid, yet the thought of Anita with another man made his insides clench. Pushing aside that line of thinking, he turned back to her. "Harris doesn't look that old. He's an ex-SEAL and a strong guy. Forget it. I was just fishing for information that might help you." *Yeah, right.*

She sighed and settled into the sofa. "I'm the second owner of this condo. I thought maybe the previous owners had hidden something, like in a crime show where jewels or bodies are hidden in the walls." She laughed softly. "I watch too many crime shows. But since I had the place totally renovated, I know there's nothing hidden in the walls or under the floors."

"Has anyone given you something lately? Maybe that guy you dated."

Frowning, she met his gaze. "John was very generous to me, even after I told him to stop giving me so many gifts. He always had interesting stuff at his shop, and whenever he found something in his travels he thought I'd like, he'd buy it for me. He was a great guy, but it felt like he was trying to buy my love."

"But you didn't love him."

"Sometimes I wish I could have, but it's not what I want. I'm perfectly happy with my life as it is." She looked down and nervously rolled the hem of her sweater between her fingers.

Luke wondered if she was trying to convince herself or him

that her life was perfect without a man. He placed his fingers under her chin. She looked up, and their eyes met. "Someday I want to find out why an intelligent, beautiful, warm woman like you feels that way. But now, we need to figure out what these people want. Why don't you show me the gifts the antiques guy gave you?" If the list was in something Sweeney gave her, it had to be a big enough item where it could be hidden without her knowing.

An hour later, they'd sifted through the jewelry John had given Anita, semi-precious stones, more expensive pieces, and quality costume jewelry, items he'd come across in his business. None were big enough to hide anything.

Anita and Luke stood in her bedroom looking down at the jewelry strewn across the bed. Standing so close to Anita, Luke was acutely aware of her warmth and smoldering sensuality.

As if she'd read his thoughts, she looked up at him. Fire sparked from her expressive eyes. Like a hundred Christmas lights, the emotion in her eyes dazzled him. Finally, he cleared his throat and stepped back, trying to diffuse the sexual tension. He had a mission. That was all.

"John got most of this jewelry at estate sales," Anita said in a calm voice. It was as if the sexual heat he'd felt hanging heavy in the room had disappeared. He wondered if he'd misread the gleam in her eyes.

"Maybe someone whose family used to own one of these pieces wants it back," she continued.

Luke shook his head. "If that were the case and they were on the up-and-up, why wouldn't they approach you and offer to buy the piece back? And if they were the ones who broke in, they would have taken the jewelry then."

She chewed her lip. "You're right."

"Did this guy sell furniture and other household goods at his shop?" Luke asked.

"Yes."

"Did he give you any pieces of furniture, something big enough to hide whatever these people might want?"

"I bought a Queen Anne desk from him. It's in my office."

"Let's look at it."

Anita emptied her desk and she and Luke took out drawers, looking for hidden compartments, but they found nothing. They faced each other. Luke wondered if the same frustration tightening her face showed on his.

"That was a dead end," she said.

He slid his hand down her arm to grasp her hand. "We'll keep working on it. You've been through enough tonight. Get some sleep. Maybe something will come to you after you're rested."

She walked him to the door. "Thanks for coming over and for helping me look," she said as she opened the door to let him out.

"We're neighbors. I'm glad to help you any way I can."

Damn, but he wanted her. *Bad idea, buddy.*

Rather than take her into his arms, he said, "Set your security alarm when I leave. Call me if anything happens. I don't care what time it is."

"Okay. Goodnight, Luke."

"Goodnight, Anita."

It was for the best that he hadn't kissed her. His mind said the words, but his body knew it lied.

◇◇◇

"What's going on?" Murray asked when he picked up Luke's call a little later.

Holding his bottle of beer in one hand and the phone in the other, Luke paced his kitchen. "Someone grabbed her outside her house tonight and tried to drag her into a car. The scumbag said they'd take her for a little ride to convince her to play ball with them."

"You gotta be shittin' me," Murray said. "They've escalated. They must be desperate. Are you any closer to finding that list or even knowing if she has it?"

Luke took a swig of beer before answering. "She says she has no idea what's going on. She showed me everything Sweeney gave her. Other than the desk, most of it is jewelry. No place to hide the list."

"What about the desk?"

"We went through the whole damn thing, tore it apart. No hidden compartments, nothing taped to the back or the bottom."

"Shit! We need that list before the syndicate gets it, Corrado."

"Don't you think I know that?"

"Keep looking. Does she trust you yet?"

"I'm getting there." Luke took another long drag on his beer, needing it to drown his frustrations. It didn't help.

"Get close to her, but not like what happened in Mexico. We don't want a repeat."

"Give me some credit, Murray. I know what I'm doing."

"I hope so, for all our sakes." Murray ended the call.

Luke threw the phone on the kitchen counter and pulled another longneck out of the refrigerator. He stalked into the living room and sank onto a chair. He had to think, to work things out. Maybe Sweeney hadn't given Anita the list after all, though the goons after her were convinced he had.

Anita. He'd wanted to kiss her tonight. Hell, he wanted to do a lot more than that. But he had to keep it cool and friendly, and he knew why. Murray hadn't had to remind him. Mexico and Maria were never far from Luke's mind.

He turned on the TV, barely noticing what was on the screen, and finished his drink. Slamming the empty bottle onto the table, he stood, stretching muscles unused to inactivity. He needed to join a gym. As dangerous as Mexico had been, he'd been deeply undercover, in the middle of the action every day, a rush that fed his need for excitement. Now, he spent his days at the Philly field office sifting through intel, working with ICE and international agencies to get the human trafficking ringleaders and put them in prison. Good work, necessary work, but sitting at a desk all day plucked his last reserve of patience.

He bent to pick up the TV remote when his phone rang, his private cell, not the secure one he used to call Murray. Unknown to the Agency at the time, he'd bought the phone in Mexico so

Maria could call him. When the Agency found he had an unauthorized phone, they'd seized it, but returned it after his assignment in Los Angeles. Only a few people, including Anita, had this number now.

Fearful something had happened to her, he retrieved the phone from the coffee table and checked the ID. His heart thudded and his pulse accelerated. Maria's number. That couldn't be. She'd died in his arms.

With trepidation, he connected the call. He kept quiet, waiting for the person on the other end to speak. Finally, a faint voice said, "Mr. Luis?"

He froze at the soft female voice speaking Spanish. Maria had never known his real name. His caller didn't know it either. "Yes," he replied in Spanish.

"Mr. Luis, I have…"

The call disconnected. Luke stared down at the phone. He quickly returned the call and got an automated voice telling him to leave a message. He hung up.

Who the hell would be using Maria's phone? Was this a trick to pull out his real identity? He needed to watch his back. Mendoza had killed Maria, and he wanted Luke dead.

CHAPTER SEVEN

Her house had never looked better. Anita stood in the living room perusing the upscale Christmas decorations Elaine's design team had put up all through the first floor. They'd used tasteful designs in gold and red, giving the place a festive look that belonged in a decorating magazine. The clean scent of pine wafted from the huge fir tree standing in a corner of the living space. The tree was festooned with red lights, gold glass balls, and gold streamers—a work of art. Anita had good taste, and the interior designer she'd hired to help furnish her house had done a great job, but Elaine's people had taken it to a new level.

Anita walked around, stopping to sniff the fresh flower arrangements and running her hands over the smooth wood of the inlaid tables the designers had set up. The pops of color in the decorations complemented the gray and white color scheme of her place. The dark gray of her leather sofa and chairs stood out against the pale gray walls and white trim. She'd always found the gray and white calming. And God knew, with her hectic life, calm was good.

The catering staff bustled about putting the final touches on the presentation of the food set up in the dining room. The delicious aromas of Beef Wellington, duck l'orange and other gourmet food she didn't recognize mingled with the tree's pine scent and bayberry from the candles placed throughout the rooms. Surprisingly, the eclectic scents worked well together and contributed to the homey yet elegant Christmas atmosphere.

The wait staff stood by, ready to go into action as soon as the first guest arrived. One of the waiters held up a flute of champagne to her. When she nodded, he brought it over. Anita sipped, grateful for the coolness of the liquid, wishing for the hundredth time she'd hadn't felt trapped and manipulated into allowing Elaine the use of her home.

She expected the Cutfords any minute. Feeling she needed moral support, she'd invited Jo, Franco, and Luke.

In the three days since her attack outside her condo, Harris had kept watch over her during the day while she was at work. Luke called her every night after she got home to be sure she was okay, but she hadn't seen him. He'd said he was busy at work, but she'd picked up a tone of evasiveness in his voice. She suspected he had secrets. After Kent, she'd learned to hold onto a healthy dose of mistrust.

For now, she'd put aside her misgivings and her fears. She'd allowed Luke to get close, and she needed to keep her distance from him, for her heart's sake. But she'd wanted him here tonight. Christmas was coming, her favorite holiday. Truth be told, it was also her loneliest, although she looked forward to her family's annual Christmas Eve party. But Christmas Eve was a few weeks away. Tonight, she had to survive the Cutfords and their friends.

Catching a glimpse of herself in the large mirror that hung over the sofa, she ran her free hand over her hair. Justin had given her an elegant upsweep. He was quickly gaining a reputation as one of the city's top stylists. Other salons were after him. However, he wanted to stay with Anita—partner with her—but she didn't know if she could give up total control.

True, she needed a break from her killing hours. A partner made sense, but what would she do with the extra time? She had no husband, no children, really didn't want a family. Her stomach clenched with the lie. In the deepest recesses of her soul, she longed for what Doriana and Jo had—husbands who adored them, children, the whole white-picket-fence dream. But it wasn't for her and it was better not to long for what she couldn't have.

Pushing her thoughts away, Anita rubbed the large ruby pendent hanging on a thick gold chain around her neck. Like a worry bead, it calmed her. The ruby perfectly matched her body-hugging short red sheath and three-inch red stilettos. John had given her the ruby, and she wore it tonight to honor him and his memory.

The doorbell rang, startling her. She jerked her hand holding the champagne flute. A little of the liquid sloshed over the side of her glass onto the floor. One of the wait staff rushed over with a napkin and blotted the liquid off the pale hardwood.

She drew a deep breath. Show time. Much as she dreaded this party, she'd look at it as a business meeting. Many influential people, the cream of Philadelphia society, would be here. Most were already her clients, but she'd have a chance to gain new ones with the Cutfords' connections. Plastering a welcoming smile on her face, she waited while the butler hired for the occasion went to the door.

"Darling, you look amazing." Elaine Cutford, wearing one of her mink coats, waltzed through the door and glided smoothly toward Anita. Her husband followed in her wake. Elaine's diamond chandelier earrings sparkled with her movements, catching the light from the candles.

"Thanks, Elaine."

Elaine hugged her and gave her air kisses. One of the waiters hurried over to take Elaine's mink and Mace's black overcoat.

Anita stepped back and scanned Elaine. "You look amazing, too."

"Thanks, darling." Elaine grabbed a flute of champagne from a tray held by one of the servers.

Wearing a short, exquisitely cut black silk dress that looked couture, and black high-heeled sandals, her legs bare, and her long red-blonde hair flowing down her back, Elaine looked twenty years younger than the fifty she sometimes admitted to.

"You're beautiful, as always," Mace said to Anita. He grabbed her hand and pulled her into a tight hug. He held on a little too long, and Anita gently extricated herself. Mace, tall, silver-haired, tanned, athletic, in his late fifties, was the epitome of the supernova, self-made multi-millionaire. He came on to Anita almost every time she was with the Cutfords. If Anita were to believe the rumors, the Cutfords each took lovers on a regular basis. Several times, Anita had seen Elaine at high-end restaurants snuggling up to well-built young men.

How they lived wasn't Anita's to judge. If she were to ever get married, she'd demand total loyalty from her husband. And she'd give him the same too.

A waiter came by with more champagne. Mace took a glass, and the trio headed farther into the living room.

"The place looks gorgeous," Elaine said. "I told you Milano does a terrific job. You should hire him to redecorate your place."

Anita let Elaine's slight put-down roll over her. She liked her place. Her decorator had made sure it reflected Anita's tastes—clean and modern.

The other guests started arriving, and Anita had no more time to think. Occasionally, she'd glance at the wall clock, wondering when Luke would arrive. Forced to make nice with people she considered insufferable snobs, she needed him there. She looked with relief toward the door when Jo and Franco arrived. Jo had been to Anita's salon earlier that day, and Justin had put her auburn hair into a casual upsweep with tendrils left loose to touch her shoulders. Wearing an emerald green dress that perfectly matched her sparkling eyes, she was one of the most beautiful women Anita had ever seen. Her pregnancy only made her more beautiful.

Anita hurried over to greet them. "Jo, you look gorgeous." She hugged her cousin-in-law.

"You are stunning," Jo said, standing back to look at Anita.

"What about me? Don't I look sexy?" Franco said with a grin.

Anita laughed. "Franco, you're as beautiful as ever, but then you know that."

Grinning, he gave her a quick hug.

Waving a hand, Anita said, "Go mingle, have some food and drinks. Everything is delicious."

She looked toward the door as the butler opened it for another guest. Luke entered the room, walking with the easy grace of a panther. Blinking, Anita stood frozen. Luke's beauty stole her breath. His black suit and snowy white shirt, worn tieless, the first few buttons undone, showed off the perfection of his bronzed skin and muscular body. His close-cropped black hair emphasized his high cheekbones and full lips.

"Wow!" His admiring gaze raked her as he approached. "You look...wow!"

"Thanks. You look pretty hot yourself."

He shot her a wicked grin and leaned closer to whisper in her ear. "Let's get out of here and go back to my place." His eyes smoldered, sinful as the richest chocolate.

Heat suffused her and she stepped back. "Stop kidding."

"Sweetheart, I'm serious."

She laughed, trying to dissolve the sensual awareness that rocked her. He tempted her, made her want to ditch the party and go with him, to explore that muscled body of his. He tempted her in other ways too. She'd kept protective barriers around her heart for so long. Yet, her spirit yearned for intimacy with Luke, to let him into her life, to know him, all of him, in every way.

Pushing aside her fears and her desires, Anita turned toward the table laden with food. "Let's eat. I've been so nervous all day, I haven't eaten much." A stomach full of food might help her get over her need for Luke. *Yeah, sure.*

Later, all the guests had arrived and the party was in full swing. Soft music from the sound system the Cutfords' team had set up played in the background. Anita stood still, letting the soothing music calm her. She looked over at Luke, who was in conversation with Jo and Franco. She was glad to see Luke getting along so well with her family. Anita suspected he didn't like the Cutfords' friends any better than Franco and Jo did. Or she did.

"Who is that six feet of Latin hotness?" Elaine said, coming up to Anita and nodding toward Luke. "Where have you been hiding him?"

Anita bristled as an unwanted surge of jealousy spiked through her. She wanted to tell Elaine that Luke was hands-off, but she had no hold on him. She figured Luke was in his late thirties, maybe forty. Too old for Elaine. She took a large swallow of champagne, washing down her disgust at her own mean thoughts. So not like her.

Forcing a cordial smile, she said, "His name is Luke Corrado and he's my new neighbor. I would have introduced you, but I didn't see you when he came in."

Elaine waved a hand. "Don't worry. I'll introduce myself." A calculating gleam had come into Elaine's eyes as she studied Luke. "Is he a neighbor with benefits?"

"No, it's not like that."

"Pity." Elaine laughed. "If he were my neighbor, I'd be on him like whipped cream on strawberries. Excuse me while I go talk to your *neighbor*."

Hips swaying, the older woman slinked toward Luke. Unable to watch Elaine flirt with him, Anita turned away. Feeling the need to be alone, free from the self-absorbed people crowding her downstairs, she headed upstairs.

In the doorway to her bedroom, she stopped and gasped. Mace Cutford was going through her dresser drawers. Her shock turned to anger that boiled into a storm in her gut. Muscles tight, she stepped into the room. "Mace, what are you doing?"

He straightened and turned to her, a sheepish grin on his face. "Anita! Elaine was feeling chilled and asked me to see if you had a wrap she could use."

Anita folded her arms across her chest and shot him a narrow-eyed look. "Why didn't you ask me?"

His smile reminded Anita of a snake. Still smiling, he strode toward her. "We didn't want to bother you." His voice had gotten husky. He reached out to touch her ruby pendant. His hand brushed the tops of her breasts.

Disgust knotted in her chest. She swallowed bile and backed away.

"Nice pendant." His eyes darkened and he looked at her chest. "You look sexy as hell, as always." He moved closer.

She stepped back and hit the doorframe. Trapped. She suppressed a gag at the smell of whiskey coming from him.

"Quit playing hard to get. Let me take care of you," he said in that same husky voice. "I can make your life easy and glamorous, set you up in a penthouse on Rittenhouse Square. Take you around the world. You'll never want for anything again."

"Stop it, Mace. Elaine is my friend. I've told you to leave me alone."

He touched the pendant again and skimmed his fingers along the tops of her breasts.

She tried to twist away, but he had her pinned. She lifted her leg, prepared to kick him in the groin.

"You heard the lady. Get away from her."

Mace jumped back.

Freed, Anita jerked around to see Luke in the hallway. She gave him a grateful smile.

"Hey, man, I didn't mean anything." Mace lifted his hands in a surrender gesture. "I was just kidding. It's what I do. Right, Anita?"

"You'd better go downstairs Mace," she said.

"Sure. Anything you say."

He reminded her of a dog turning tail and running away.

"You okay?" Luke took her hand and pulled her to face him. "Did that jerk hurt you?"

"No. I can usually handle Mace. He's always coming on to me. Elaine's my friend so I put up with him."

"You shouldn't have to put up with that."

"They've been good to me. I owe them. They never forget their friends. Or their enemies. I don't want to be on their enemies' list. I guess it's the cost of doing business to put up with both of them from time-to-time."

Nodding toward her room, she said, "We need to talk." She pulled him inside, shut the door, and faced him. "Luke, I found Mace going through one of my dresser drawers."

"You're kidding. Did he say why?"

"He said Elaine sent him up here to look for a wrap for her. It's strange, don't you think?"

"Very. Let's get back to your guests, but I'll keep an eye on Cutford for you."

◇◇◇

Twenty minutes later, Luke sipped his wine and watched Cutford from across the room. The man seemed like your ordinary big shot businessman, arrogant and smug, the kind with more money than brains. Cutford flirted with the women and held court with the men, most of whom seemed to hang onto his every word. Luke had run across many men like Cutford in his line of work and hadn't much use for them.

As soon as he could, he'd call Murray and ask him to run a check on Cutford. The intel Sweeney passed on said the leader of the crime syndicate was in Philly. Cutford didn't look like the type, but Luke had learned appearances could be deceiving. He'd been putting in long hours at headquarters, but they weren't any closer than they'd been when Sweeney disappeared, and the list with him. The Agency had to check every suspicious person, regardless of his standing in the community.

Laughter from the other end of the room jerked his attention to Anita. She stood with her cousin and his wife, laughing at something one of them said. God, she was beautiful, with that thick black hair. His fingers itched to release it from that upsweep until the strands flowed down her back. Her naked back.

His body came to attention at the thought of her luscious body under his. *Down, guy.*

He grabbed a tiny crab cake from a waiter and popped it into his mouth, hoping the food would tamp down his raging libido. It didn't work. He suspected the only cure for his desire was to make love to Anita. Yet, one night with her would never be enough.

A little past two o'clock, the guests started to drift out. Luke strolled to where Anita stood talking with a couple who were preparing to leave. He slipped his arm around her waist when he reached the group. He couldn't understand it, but something inside him compelled him to stake his claim, to declare Anita was his. When she looked at him, the awareness shining from her eyes matched his and touched a chord of longing deep within him.

Finally, all the guests had left and he was alone with her. He'd been determined to stay until the last guest had gone. He had to be sure she was okay. And, if he were honest with himself, he didn't want to leave her.

She'd kicked off her shoes and stood at the door with him. Without the three-inch heels she barely came to his shoulder. He wanted to gather her into his arms and protect her, the way he hadn't protected Sofia or Maria.

He skimmed a finger over the faint dark circles under her eyes. "You look tired. Get some rest. Tomorrow's Sunday so you can sleep in. Take care of yourself."

She sighed. "Thanks. I am tired. I worked all day, and even though the caterers took care of everything, as hostess I had to be on duty for the whole party."

Her full lips parted, inviting him to taste her. He bent and brushed a soft kiss on that appealing mouth.

She wound her arms around his neck and pressed her lush body closer. Luke cradled the back of her head and deepened the kiss, sliding his tongue into her soft moistness.

After several passion-filled minutes, they pulled away. Her eyes were huge, the pupils dilated. He wanted to carry her up the stairs and make wild, passionate love to her all night.

"I guess I'd better go," he ground out.

Did he imagine the disappointment in her eyes?

She gave him a small smile. "Good night, Luke, and thanks for coming to my rescue earlier with Mace, and for being here for me tonight."

He brushed back strands of hair from her face and rubbed his thumbs gently over her cheekbones. "Any time, sweetheart."

His hand on the doorknob, he said, "Lock up after I leave and set your security alarm."

"I will."

He slipped out and walked the few feet to his door. Anita had gotten to him, had worked her way into his heart, the heart he thought would never heal after Maria. The thought of losing himself to another woman scared him almost as much as facing Mendoza.

CHAPTER EIGHT

"I don't think the bitch has the list, boss. Sweeney must have passed it to someone else."

"She has it. You fucked up, you and your men. You should have nabbed her the other day. With a little persuasion, she would have told us where it is. I can't depend on any of you. I'll have to do it myself."

Gordon paced his boss's living room, unable to look into those ice blue eyes. When the boss got that look, it meant someone was in big trouble. He didn't want it to be him. Fighting to control his fears, he whirled around. "Look, boss, give us another chance. We didn't know she had security. We'll be ready next time. Me and the boys will get that list. The Feds don't have it, and we're not sure they even know about it. If they had it, we'd all be in jail now."

Face red with anger, the boss strode up to him and poked him in the chest with a long finger. "One more time, Gordon. You get that list or you end up in the Delaware like Sweeney."

◇◇◇

The doorbell ringing jerked Anita from a sound sleep. Groggy, she struggled to sit up and pushed hair back from her face. Bright sunlight streamed between the gaps in the curtains. A glance at the bedside clock told her it was nearly ten. She never slept this late, but she'd been wiped out after the party last night.

The bell sounded again, more urgent this time, propelling her out of bed. She threw on a silk robe and jammed her feet into slippers. Tying the belt on her robe, she hurried down the stairs.

When she looked through the door's peephole, a smiling

Luke stood on the landing holding up a bag from the bakery at the nearby strip mall. Pleasure zapped her, making her pulse jump. Before disengaging the security system, she leaned against the door, trying to calm her racing pulse. She hadn't known Luke long, but through his caring and generosity, he'd found his way into her heart. She rubbed her forehead. No, that wouldn't happen.

The doorbell rang again and she hurriedly disengaged the alarm. She'd let him into her house, but not her heart. Never her heart.

"Morning, Sleeping Beauty," he said when she let him in. "Took you long enough. You okay?"

"Still a little groggy, I guess."

"I thought you might like breakfast." He held up the bag again.

"That's really sweet of you, but you didn't have to buy me breakfast."

He leaned closer and gave her a wicked grin. "No one's ever called me sweet before. I'm far from that."

She laughed. "Sweet and spicy. Is that better?"

"Much. Let's eat."

She followed him into the kitchen and took plates and mugs down from the cabinets and set them on the center island. "I don't usually sleep this late."

"You had a big day and night."

"And I'm glad it's over."

"Sit. I'll make coffee." He shook the bag. "I didn't know what you liked so I got us an assortment."

"You're too good to me." The words slipped out.

His intense gaze held hers. She read desire in their depths, and something else, something that reached into the deepest recesses of her soul, the place where she kept her true hopes hidden.

"I can make the coffee." She turned away and started towards the coffee maker.

He grabbed her arm, stopping her. "Get back here. I'll take

care of it."

Thirty minutes later, their stomachs filled with fresh-baked pastries and strong coffee, they sat on stools around her kitchen island. Anita sighed and patted her belly. "That was delicious. Thank you." She glanced at the clock and gasped. "The cleaning crew Elaine hired will be here any minute. I've got to get dressed." She jumped down from the stool and began collecting the empty plates and mugs.

Luke took the dishes from her. "The cleaning crew will take care of this. Get dressed. I'll let them in."

"Thanks, Luke." She jogged out of the kitchen.

◇◇◇

The cleaning crew consisted of five women, four who sounded American and one with a thick Russian or Eastern European accent. The intel the Agency had received from Sweeney and their informers said the leader of the human trafficking cartel was Eastern European. While Anita showered and dressed, Luke kept an eye on the cleaners, especially the Russian.

The American women chatted and laughed as they cleaned the kitchen. The Russian woman threw furtive glances around the room and kept quiet. Luke sat in the dining area, supposedly reading the Sunday paper, but his attention stayed on the women. At the sound of breaking glass, one of the women began shouting at the others.

Luke ran into the kitchen to see two wine glasses shattered on the tiled floor. The women signaled to him they had everything under control. As he turned to leave, he realized the Russian wasn't in the room. She must have slipped out when he ran in.

Senses on alert, he hurried through the empty living area to Anita's study, tucked into an alcove in the spacious loft. The Russian was there, frantically searching through the drawers in the antique desk Anita had gotten from Sweeney.

"What are you doing?" Luke asked, striding toward her.

The woman jerked her head up and took a step back. "I dust this desk."

"You didn't look like you were dusting." He wanted to grab her by the throat and force the truth from her. But he couldn't blow his cover. "What are you looking for?"

"I look for nothing," she said, raising her chin in a defiant gesture.

He scanned her, but saw nothing in her hands. "Empty your pockets."

"You have no right."

"Empty them now or I'll call the police."

With a snarl and a look filled with hate, she pulled out the linings in her pants pockets, showing him they were empty.

"All of them," he said, nodding toward the smock she wore over her clothes. She shoved her hands into the pockets. One hand came up empty, but in the other she held an antique pearl-handled letter opener.

"Give it to me." Luke held out his hand.

She held the opener like a weapon. The malice in her eyes said she meant to use it on him. Luke took a fight stance and shot her a glare that dared her to try. After a seconds-long stare down, she blinked and thrust the opener into his open palm.

"Now get out of here," he said.

"I wait for the others. I need ride."

"You can wait for them outside."

She scurried out the front door.

◇◇◇

"Tell boss I no find anything."

Nina's heavily accented voice coming through the phone sent fear rocketing through Gordon. The boss would not be happy.

"You had a lot of time to search that fucking house. What the hell happened?"

"That boyfriend of the woman's. He watched me. And he threw me out."

"Shit! We need to get rid of him." Gordon disconnected the call and slipped the phone back into his pocket. He'd spent a lot of money greasing the palm of the cleaning company's owner to get Nina on the crew. And she couldn't deliver. As he walked along Market Street, sweat beaded his forehead despite the December cold. Time was running out. The boss wanted that list. The Santisi bitch had it. Sweeney had said her name right before he died.

◇◇◇

Anita closed her front door after Luke left and leaned against it. He had stayed at her place most of the day, saying he enjoyed her company. But she'd noticed an edge to him, as if he was on guard, waiting. It scared the crap out of her, but when she'd asked him, he'd merely smiled and said her tight nerves had her imagining things.

A knock at her door made her jump. She hadn't reset her security system yet, but expecting Luke, she opened it without checking the peephole. "Did you forget—?" She let out a scream as two men wearing ski masks pushed their way in. One of the men grabbed her and twisted her arms behind her back.

"Shut your mouth or I will kill you," he growled.

He pushed her into the living room while the second intruder stood watch at the door. The first man threw her onto the sofa and leaned toward her. With garlic-laced breath, he said, "You can make this real easy, girlie. We know the dude gave you something. You give it to us and we let you live."

"Dude?" she said on a shaky whisper.

The guy grabbed her chin and squeezed, bringing tears to her eyes. "Where the fuck is it?"

"I don't know what you're talking about."

"I don't have time for games, bitch."

His beady gray eyes impaled her. Her limbs shook. Her vision clouded. A sudden fierce will to live kicked in. He stood close, too close for his own good. She kicked him in the groin. He yelped and fell back.

She jumped from the sofa. The second guy ran over and tackled her. They tumbled to the floor. He pushed her facedown against the Berber carpet and placed a hand on her back, between her shoulder blades.

The rapid beating of her heart echoed in the quiet room. They were going to kill her. She squirmed, trying to get free, but he pressed his hand harder on her back.

"Bitch!" The first guy had recovered and strolled over. His thick black boots were inches from her face. He grabbed a hunk of her hair and pulled. "You'll pay for that."

The second man released her, and the first one, still holding her hair, yanked her to her feet. She cried out in pain. Darting her eyes between them, she had to think fast. The walls between her place and Luke's were thin. Forcing down her fear, Anita raised her head and screamed.

The first guy slapped her hard across the face. Her head snapped back and she tasted blood.

Within minutes, her partially-opened front door crashed against the wall as Luke ran in and threw himself at the guy closest to him. Fists flying, they went down. Still held by the second man, Anita kicked him in the shins. He loosened his grip and she jerked free. She ran to the phone with him in hot pursuit. He grabbed for her. Then Luke was there, pulling him off her. The first man lay prone on the floor where Luke had left him.

With shaky fingers, she dialed 911. "Home invasion," she shouted into the phone.

The intruder Luke had fought staggered to his feet and ran out the door. Luke had the second guy in a strangle hold. With a loud grunt and an elbow to Luke's stomach, the man broke loose and followed his partner.

Breathing heavily, blood coming from a cut on his lip, his face scratched, Luke ran to her and gathered her into his arms.

"It's okay, baby. It's okay," he crooned.

CHAPTER NINE

The police had taken their statements and left. Luke made Anita a cup of tea, and they sat together on the sofa sipping their drinks.

He gave Anita a small smile and swept strands of her hair back to tuck them behind her ears. "Feeling better?"

Calmness stole over her at his touch, and she nodded.

"At least your door isn't broken this time," he said. "Good thing the goons left it open or I would have had to break it down."

"You could have blasted through the walls for all I care. Thank you. You're a true friend." She drank some tea and rested her head on the back of the sofa. The hot, sweet slide of the drink as it went down her throat soothed her almost as much as Luke's closeness.

"Haven't had too many women call me a friend." He chuckled. "Other names, of course, but not friend." He set down his mug to lean closer. "You're sure the guy said the *dude* gave you something?"

"Yes."

"And you don't know what he was talking about?"

She sat straighter. "No. If I knew what they wanted or who the *dude* is, I'd be more than happy to give it to them."

Anita tried to smile, but couldn't. "I hate to think what would have happened if you hadn't come in when you did."

Anger sparked from his eyes. "Let's not think about that. I'm glad I'm close enough to help." He studied her. "Maybe I should move in with you until the police catch the guys who are after you."

Anita slid away, putting distance between them. From the intense look in his eyes, he was serious. "Thanks for the offer, Luke, and I am very grateful to have you close. But I can't have you live with me."

"I don't want anything to happen to you." He grasped her shoulders. "In a short time, I've come to care for you."

Fear that had nothing to do with her attack rose up. Either Luke was a smooth operator or he really did care about her. Somehow she believed he cared. That wasn't the way things were meant to be, at least not in her world.

Not trusting herself so close to him, she pulled free. "Luke, I really like you, but I'm not ready for anything other than friendship right now."

"I understand. And as your friend, I worry about you." His tender smile brought out the dimple she was coming to love and confirmed the truth of his words.

"You have to promise you'll be more careful," he said. "No opening that door until you've checked who's outside. Understood?"

"Yes. If you hadn't just left, I wouldn't have assumed it was you at the door."

"Don't assume anything anymore."

"Got it." Despite her protests, a wave of pleasure swept over her that Luke cared enough about her to worry about her safety.

◇◇◇

Gordon and the two men he'd sent to get the Santisi bitch drove to the warehouse off Delaware Avenue where the boss liked to conduct business. Fear hung heavy inside the car. Gordon knew plenty of men who'd been summoned to the warehouse, never to be heard from again. They'd tortured Sweeney there. Gordon had enjoyed that. He hated the Feds. However, he feared he wouldn't enjoy being at the warehouse this time.

They parked the car and made their way over the cobblestones to the cavernous building. The squeak of rats in the dark made him shiver. Gordon and the men slipped through the door into a mostly empty room with windows high up and chains hanging from the ceiling. Sweeney hung on those chains for days before he finally died. The sucker had been stronger than they'd thought.

The slap of shoe leather on cement announced the arrival of their boss. The men turned around.

"Want to tell me why the bitch isn't with you?" the boss asked.

"Boss, they had her, but that guy what's been hanging around heard her scream." Gordon forced himself to remain calm. He'd learned long ago not to show fear to the boss.

The men with him nodded like bobble-head dolls. Gordon could smell their fear. He knew the boss could too.

"What did the guy who worked you over look like?" the boss asked.

"Tall, Hispanic," Leroy, one of the men, answered.

"And both of you couldn't fight off one man?" the boss asked calmly, too calmly.

Gordon stood rooted to the spot.

"Imbeciles," the boss screamed. "I want that bitch. Sweeney said her name before he died. He had to have given her the fucking list. Find it."

Gordon ran a finger under the collar of his shirt. "We'll get her, boss."

The boss's eyes turned that icy blue Gordon had come to dread. He backed away.

"Shoot them," the boss shouted to someone who stood in the shadows.

Two shots rang out and the men with Gordon dropped. Blood stained the fronts of their shirts and flowed onto the floor.

"Leroy was my cousin," Gordon screamed.

"I don't give a fuck if it was your mother. One more chance, Gordon," the boss said. "Fail and you won't die quickly like them. Now get the hell out."

Gordon slunk away, but hate and revenge went with him. He'd make the boss pay for killing his cousin.

◇◇◇

The black beady eyes of death stared down at Luke. Mendoza laughed, a sound of pure evil that reverberated off the walls of the cabin. With a devil's grin, Mendoza slipped his knife from the sheath around his waist and held it up. The dim light from the one bulb hanging from the ceiling glinted on the blade. Luke prepared to die.

With a strangled gasp, Luke jerked awake. He sat up and threw the covers off. Wiping sweat from his brow, he glanced at the clock. Two in the morning. He'd finally fallen asleep after hours of tossing, but the dreams started. The damn dreams. He thought he'd put that behind him. This new mission, his fear that he couldn't protect Anita, had brought the nightmares back.

Things were closing in on the Agency and Anita. The crime organization was getting more desperate. The attack on Anita yesterday had proved that.

His secure cell rang and he grabbed it from his nightstand. "Don't you ever sleep, Murray?" he said into the phone.

"No, and it doesn't look like you do either. We finished our investigation of Cutford."

Luke straightened. "And you had to call me at this ungodly hour to tell me?"

"Watch the snark, Corrado. You're on the clock 24/7. Remember that."

"What did you find?"

"Nothing. Nada. Mace Cutford was born in Boston. He has no Eastern European ties. Seems like exactly what he is—a jackass millionaire with more money than brains."

"There's more to him than that. My instincts are telling me to watch the guy."

Murray chuckled. "You saying that because of your feeling or because he laid a hand on your girl?"

"She's not my girl, but she is my responsibility."

"Be careful." Murray's voice softened. "She's a job, nothing more. Neither of us wants a repeat of Mexico. I smoothed that one over for you. I can't do it again."

"I know, Murray, and I owe you." Murray had kept Luke's

real involvement with Maria out of the reports. Agents weren't supposed to fall in love with the women they were investigating. Luke had broken that cardinal rule, and Maria had paid with her life.

"About that tail you want on the woman," Murray continued. Luke had called him earlier to tell him about the attack on Anita yesterday and to request the Agency put a tail on her. "No can do. We're stretched thin. Big trouble at the Mexican border, a major drug bust. If she didn't already have private security, I'd have to pull some strings to free up our guys, but she's covered. You're responsible for her when she's home."

"I understand. I'll handle my end. I don't think she'll be opening her door to strangers any time soon."

"Take care and watch your back." Murray disconnected.

Luke shifted his position on the bed, his mind going over everything that had happened to Anita. Had Sweeney talked before he died? Had he told his captors he'd given the list to her? If he had, he didn't tell them *how* he'd given it to her or Anita would be dead already and the list in the wrong hands. The thought briefly crossed his mind that Sweeney had told her about the list and Anita was playing with the Agency while she tried to sell the list to the highest bidder. He dismissed that idea almost the minute it entered his head. He could read people. Anita had no idea what was going on around her.

His personal cell phone rang and he grabbed it off the nightstand. His breath hitched. Maria's number.

He connected the call. "Who is this?" he asked in Spanish.

That same tentative, soft female voice said in quivering Spanish, "Mr. Luis. I cannot talk long. They're watching. They know. You must come. They will kill him."

"What the hell? Who will kill who?"

He heard a rustle, then silence. Luke stared at the phone as if he could will it to ring again.

He'd trusted Maria even though the Agency felt sure she knew about her brother's operations. But Maria had been naïve and innocent. And now Maria was dead. He'd held her lifeless body. Luke had loved her. He'd also killed her.

Yet her phone was still in service. The strange woman with the oddly familiar voice had sounded frightened. How the hell could he help when he had no idea what was going on?

He jumped from the bed and paced the room. Mexico was behind him, Maria gone, her brother still at large. Her brother's men would have killed him too if Murray's agents hadn't gotten there when they did.

They had to have left something undone in Mexico. Was Mendoza behind the strange phone calls, using them to ferret Luke out into the open?

CHAPTER TEN

The day after Anita was attacked in her home, Elaine Cutford sat at her station at the salon getting her hair done. "I want the 411 on that hot neighbor of yours. He looks tasty. How can you resist that hunk of deliciousness?"

Disgust and unwanted jealousy left a bitter taste in Anita's mouth. Elaine was her best client and her friend, but she didn't want the other woman getting her well-manicured talons into Luke. She hadn't told Elaine about her attack and didn't intend to. Talking about it upset her too much. Besides, Elaine didn't like to discuss what she called "serious shit." She liked to talk about fashion, hair, manicures, hunky men.

Anita turned off the dryer and met Elaine's assessing green gaze in the mirror. "There's not a lot to tell. I met Luke when he moved in a few weeks ago. He's a nice guy, but I don't know much about him." She turned on the dryer again and concentrated on blowing Elaine's mass of hair, careful not to dislodge the pricey extensions.

"What type work does he do?" Elaine asked.

Why do you want to know? The words were on the tip of Anita's tongue. Elaine usually didn't give a fig about what type work a guy did, only that he was good-looking, built, and available for sex. Anita quashed her annoyance at the other woman. Used to Elaine's inquisitive nature, her questions usually didn't bother Anita. And she usually couldn't care less what guys Elaine set her sights on.

Except for this time.

Finished with Elaine's hair, Anita turned off the dryer and

set it on its stand. "Luke used to own a software company and sold it. Now he consults with other software companies."

"Interesting." Elaine's eyes glowed with a feral gleam. "He must be wealthy. Sexy, gorgeous, and wealthy." She gave a throaty laugh. "Now that's a combination I can sink my teeth and everything else into."

Anita shrugged. "I guess he's rich. I didn't think about it."

"Of course, you wouldn't, darling." Elaine studied herself in the mirror and patted her hair. "You're a genius with hair." She pushed up from her chair. "You and that yummy neighbor must come to dinner at our place very soon."

"Thanks. That sounds like fun," Anita lied. Why would she drag Luke into a pit of vipers?

◇◇◇

Two nights after the Cutfords' party and the day after Anita was attacked, Luke was cleaning up the remnants of his takeout meal when his secure cell rang.

As soon as he connected the call, Murray said, "Just checking to be sure private detail is still on the Santisi woman."

"They'll be on her until we get our hands on that list and make sure she's okay." The phone to his ear, Luke walked to the garbage bin and disposed of the food containers. "I wish there was some way we could bring the security firm in on this."

"You can't blow your cover, Corrado."

"Yeah, yeah. I know that." He exhaled deeply and sank onto one of the stools that rimmed the center island. Guilt nagged at him. He had to report the phone calls from Mexico.

"There's something else, Murray."

"I'm listening."

"I've gotten two calls from Maria's phone on my private cell, the one I brought back from Mexico."

Murray snorted. "The one you weren't supposed to have. You're lucky I saved your ass on that one."

"Yeah. Don't remind me."

"Maria's dead and her phone's still on? It's her brother. He's trying to force you out."

"That's what I think, too, yet, there's something about this woman's voice that sounds truly desperate."

"It's a woman, you say?"

"Yeah. Sounds like an older woman. Speaking Spanish. The voice is vaguely familiar. I've been wondering if it's Adelina, Maria's duenna, but I never had much interaction with her. She made herself scarce when I was around."

"What does she say?"

"That some guy's going to be killed. She calls me Mr. Luis."

"I'll check with my contact there, see if any of our agents' covers have been blown. At least she doesn't know who you really are if she calls you Luis. You tell me the next time you get one of those calls. I don't want you going rogue on us again. We might not be able to save your sorry ass next time."

"Point taken. I'll keep you informed."

"And, Corrado, don't even think of going to Mexico. The cartel has a price on your head. Understood?"

"Understood."

The line went dead. Luke slammed his phone onto the counter. This damned inactivity was getting to him. He should be grateful at least the Agency hadn't fired him after his screw-up when he'd disobeyed orders. He had Murray to thank. Rumor had it that Murray had once fallen in love with a woman who had ties to organized crime, a woman he'd been sent to guard. Murray seemed to understand the men and women working for him were human and prone to love people they shouldn't.

Luke tried to picture Maria, but her face was fading from his memory. She'd had thick black hair, like Anita's, but Maria's was curly where Anita's was straight. Maria smiled and laughed a lot when they were together.

Needing a cold brew, he got up and strode to the refrigerator, his mind on Maria. Nursing his beer, he sat back at the center island, but Anita's face intruded on his musings. Where Maria had been needy, clinging to him, dependent on him, Anita was strong, a woman who could take care of herself. She ran one of the top salon spas in Philadelphia, not an easy feat. The Agency had checked her out thoroughly when Sweeney had gotten involved with her. There was nothing in her background to indicate she had ties with the international human trafficking ring Luke had been investigating for the past five years.

He rolled his neck to loosen the tight muscles. Why the hell would Sweeney put her in jeopardy like this? How the hell had he passed the list off to her?

Luke picked up his phone and checked the time. Almost nine. What was Anita doing now? His body hardened thinking about her. He wanted her. He'd loved Maria, but he'd never felt this overwhelming need for her, a need that pulsed through him every time he got near Anita. Maria had been a virgin, soft and yielding, and would do anything he asked. She'd been far from strong, emotionally and physically.

Despite Anita's sophistication and strength, he detected tenderness and sadness within her. He wanted to explore that warmth she tried to hide, to peel away her layers and find Anita's sweet, soft core.

Someone had hurt her. Probably a man. If he ever met the guy, he'd jam his fist into the guy's face. Whatever had happened, Anita had built a wall around her heart.

Shit! He was thinking too much. A couple hours of mindless TV would take him away from his thoughts. As he strode into the living room, he knew nothing would take his mind from Anita.

CHAPTER ELEVEN

Sitting next to Luke as he drove her Mercedes through the city to the Cutfords' Rittenhouse Square penthouse, Anita sighed with contentment despite her anxiety about having dinner with the Cutfords. She'd hoped the flighty Elaine would be too busy over the holidays to invite them. No chance of that apparently. Reminding herself she had to stay on the Cutfords' good side, she'd accepted Elaine's invitation.

Anita tried to focus on the cheerful Christmas scenes unfolding past her window. Sparkling lights strung along the streets rolled by in a kaleidoscope of festive colors. The store windows were dazzling showcases of expensive goods. On a Saturday night, shoppers and others out for an evening at the theater or dining in one of the many top restaurants strolled the sidewalks. Although she wasn't looking forward to an evening with the Cutfords, Luke was with her. Somehow, he always made her feel calm, protected. Her instincts told her she was safe with him. Settling into the soft leather, she willed herself to relax and enjoy this evening.

They pulled up to the entrance of the elite apartment building and the doorman rushed down the steps to open Anita's door. Luke slipped from the driver's side and handed some bills to the parking valet who stood ready.

Luke cupped her elbow as they walked up the steps, going through the door held open by a second doorman. Once in the private elevator that would take them to the penthouse, Luke turned to Anita.

"Have I told you how beautiful you look tonight?"

She laughed. "Several times."

Elaine had directed them to dress casually. Anita wore a pair of black skinny jeans that hugged her butt, a white cashmere sweater shot with silver, and her four-inch black stiletto boots. She completed the outfit with her pale gray leather jacket.

She scanned Luke. "You look pretty good yourself."

His faded jeans showcased his long legs, and his dark blue sweater stretched across his muscular chest. Paired with his black leather jacket, a few days' stubble on his firm jaw, just enough to be sexy, he looked like a pirate come to steal her heart. But he wouldn't steal her heart because she wouldn't let him.

She almost believed the lie.

The elevator doors swooshed open to a narrow hallway. They faced the double wooden doors of the penthouse. Before they could ring the bell, Elaine, in skintight brown leather pants and a low-cut beige silk blouse, opened the door. "Come in, darlings."

Drawing Anita into the room, Elaine gave her air kisses. But she hugged Luke. Tight. Elaine's ample breasts squashed against Luke's chest.

Anita kept a smile plastered on her face, but her stomach churned. She'd seen Elaine flirt with men all the time, but she'd never openly flirted with one of Anita's boyfriends.

Mace, in pressed jeans and a blindingly white shirt, came into the room smiling, followed by Berta, their maid. Luke extricated himself from Elaine, slipped off his jacket, and handed it to the waiting maid. He turned to help Anita with hers, but Mace jumped in front of him and helped Anita out of her jacket. His hands lingered on her arms as he slipped the coat off. His wolfish smile and the gleam in his blue eyes made shivers run up her spine. Lately, he'd been bolder in his advances. She'd have to stay clear of him.

"The place looks beautiful," Anita said, following Elaine into the sunken living room with its white wool carpet over dark hardwood. A white leather sectional was flanked by brown leather chairs and a marble-slabbed coffee table. "I assume you got that wiring problem fixed."

Elaine frowned. "Wiring problem?"

"From the small fire you had, the reason you couldn't have your Christmas party here."

Laughing, Elaine ran a slim hand, the nails done in metallic green, along her hair. "Of course, darling. The fire. Everything's fine now and I've forgotten it."

Doubts rose in Anita, but she shrugged them off. She'd never known Elaine to dwell too long on anything, especially anything serious. She was too busy flitting from social event to social event, from one young guy to another, all the while obsessed with her looks and fashion.

Anita took a glass of wine proffered by Berta and let her gaze wander the room. A huge fir tree, professionally decorated in blue and silver, occupied one corner of the sprawling area. Evergreens adorned the white marble mantel above a crackling fire. The scent of pine mingled with tantalizing aromas coming from the kitchen.

"This is a great place," Luke said. "Look at that view." Holding his glass of wine, he walked out to the glass-enclosed balcony. Anita went with him and stood close as they stared out at the bright lights of the city spread below.

She'd been to the Cutfords' countless times but the view never failed to amaze her. Sighing, she looked up at Luke. "I love this view."

Luke's dimpled smile made her heart beat a little faster. Through the reflection on the glass, she caught a glimpse of Elaine and Mace watching them. The look the other couple shared, almost primitive in its intensity, made shivers crawl over Anita's skin.

A minute later, a grinning Elaine joined them on the balcony. Anita decided she must have imagined the cunning look that had passed between the Cutfords.

"How do you like the wine?" Elaine asked. "Mace just got back from Argentina where he sampled the most exquisite wines. He had cases sent up here."

"It's wonderful," Anita said. "You and Mace always have the

best of everything."

"Thank you, darling." Elaine turned to Luke. "Do you like the wine? If it's not to your taste, we can open another bottle." She ran a hand over his arm. "If there's anything you need or want, anything at all, you just let me know."

Anita resisted the urge to dump her wine over the other woman.

Luke stepped away, freeing himself from Elaine. "This is some of the best wine I've ever had. I'm good with it."

Much later, the meal over, the two couples sat on the over-sized sectional before the fire. Anita and the Cutfords drank aged brandy. Luke had declined, saying he had to drive.

"Give my compliments to your cook," Luke said to Elaine. "The meal was terrific."

Elaine gave him a flirtatious smile as her gleaming gaze trailed over him. "How do you keep that wonderful physique and still eat so heartily? Do you work out?"

He nodded. "I try to. I recently joined a gym in the city."

Anita tamped down her unreasonable jealousy and scooted a little closer to Luke. Mace sat on the other side of her, and as they'd talked, he'd inched toward her. During dinner both Cutfords had peppered Luke with questions about his background, where he went to school, what sort of software company he'd founded.

Luke handled all their questions easily. His answers had been smooth, sounding almost rehearsed, but tension had shown in the tightness of his jaw. She wondered if the other couple had noticed.

Relieved when the evening ended, she and Luke said their goodbyes. The Cutfords called for Anita's car to be brought to the front of the building. Riding down in the elevator, Luke gave Anita an appraising look.

"What?" she asked.

"How'd you get mixed up with those piranhas?"

"Piranhas?"

"If I offended you, I'm sorry, but those two aren't people I'd associate with you." He moved closer and skimmed a finger over her lips. "You're too lovable and caring for that crew."

With a nervous laugh, she stepped back, away from him and temptation. "Lovable? Me? I think there are others who won't agree with you."

He shrugged. "Then they don't see the real you."

"And you do?"

"You'd be surprised what I see."

Anita glanced away, not wanting to meet his gaze. His enigmatic remark about seeing the real her made her mind whirl. She was glad Luke was with her tonight. He made it easier to swallow the Cutfords. Yet, she sensed darkness in Luke. And truth be told, that darkness made him all the more appealing.

◇◇◇

Luke had to be careful what he said to Anita. He couldn't give anything away. But her friends *were* piranhas. There was no other name for them. The Agency couldn't find anything linking Mace Cutford to the human trafficking ring. Yet, there was a core of corruption about him and his wife. Luke had been around morally bankrupt people a long time. He'd learned to recognize the evil in others. And the goodness in others, too, like Anita.

The elevator opened on the ground floor and he stepped aside to let her exit first. It gave him a good view of her very appealing bottom and swaying hips. Her dark jeans molded to her slight frame, cupping her buttocks and showing off slim, long legs made longer by the stiletto heels she wore. Her gray leather jacket looked butter soft and expensive. He was glad she hadn't worn all black for a change.

As they walked, she turned and caught him staring. "Like what you see?" she asked in a teasing voice, echoing what he'd said when they'd met.

"I like very much." He winked at her and was rewarded with a smile.

When they got to their condos, Luke waited while Anita unlocked her door and disengaged the security alarm. He wanted to stay with her, to guard her from anyone wanting to do her

harm. And, he wanted to make love to her. Regardless of how much he desired her, she was hands-off.

"Goodnight," he said, nodding toward the alarm box. "Set that thing as soon as you get in and keep it set. I'm right next door if you need me."

"Would you like to come in for some coffee or a drink?" she asked.

"Damn, why do you have to make it so difficult for me?" His voice had taken on a husky quality.

Her brow furrowed. "What do you mean?"

He stepped closer and touched strands of her hair that lay over her shoulder, letting the silky threads slip through his fingers. "You must know I want you. I'm trying to be a good friend and not take advantage."

She laughed softly. "Do you honestly think I'd let you take advantage of me if I didn't want you to?"

"Do you want me to?"

"Yes." She spoke so quietly he wasn't sure he heard right.

"Oh, sweetheart."

"Come in." With a provocative smile, she slipped through the door and beckoned him to follow.

"What would you like to drink?" she asked after they'd shed their jackets and she'd reset the alarm. "How about Irish coffee?"

"That sounds great. I'll help. I know my way around a kitchen."

Her flirtatious smile went straight to his groin.

"There's nothing sexier than a man who knows his way around a kitchen," she said.

A while later they sat at her kitchen island sipping hot Irish coffee. Luke's gaze met Anita's.

He wanted her. Bad.

Trying to bring his libido under control, he glanced around her ultra modern open kitchen, done in shades of black, white, and gray, like the rest of the loft. The place reflected Anita's style. She reminded him of a small panther, sleek and sexy, ready with a purr or extended claws. He wanted to hear her scream his name as she climaxed.

Down, guy. He didn't know if he spoke to himself or his burgeoning erection straining against the zipper of his jeans. He sipped more coffee, welcoming the hot liquid that burned down his throat, fighting to focus his thoughts on something other than Anita squirming under him in bed. He fought a losing battle.

She wrapped one small, slender hand around her mug. Her fingernails were long and squared off, polished with pale pink. He had a sudden image of those hands wrapped around his hard cock. Her expressive golden brown eyes looked deeply into his, almost challenging. His resolve to keep her at a distance dissolved into the sexually charged atmosphere.

"Oh, hell." He stood and took her hand, pulling her up. "I want you. Now."

With an enticing smile, she wound her arms around his neck, stood on tiptoe and touched her lips to his.

He pulled her against him, letting her feel the evidence of his arousal. When she opened her mouth to him, he slipped his tongue inside. She tasted like coffee and cinnamon with a trace of whiskey. Groaning deep in his throat, his tongue explored her sweetness.

When he left her mouth to string kisses down the smooth column of her throat, she moaned softly and tilted her head back, giving herself to him. He slipped his hand under her sweater to cup one of her full breasts. The nipple hardened under his touch. He wanted to take her right then and there. She deserved better than a quickie in the kitchen.

His breathing ragged, he pulled away and met her passion-glazed eyes. "Let's take this to the bedroom."

With a nod, she grasped his hand and led him through the dining and living areas and up the steps to a long hallway with a wrought iron railing that overlooked the first floor. She pulled him inside a room at the end of the carpeted hall.

When they stepped inside, his mind barely registered the king-size bed. He gathered her into his arms.

"You're sure?" he asked.

"Very sure." Her voice was thick.

He'd never wanted her more than he did at that moment, with her tousled hair a soft halo around her face, and her generous mouth parted, inviting his possession. He backed her against the wall and took her lips in a desperate kiss that poured out his hunger and his need.

She gripped his shoulders and kissed him with the same urgency that made his blood boil. Cupping her butt, he lifted her. She wound her legs around his waist. They kissed for several lust-filled minutes. With her legs still wrapped around him and her arms twined around his neck, he carried her to the bed. When he deposited her onto the gray comforter, she looked at him with wide eyes, trusting eyes.

And he was lost.

CHAPTER TWELVE

Luke's desire wrestled with logic. This was wrong on so many levels, but right on so many more. Looking down at Anita, knowing he'd soon possess her, made a slow heat burn through him. He'd wanted her almost from the first minute he'd seen her.

Her eyes lit with gold fire and she held out her arms. "Love me, Luke."

The look in her eyes and her softly spoken words ripped away any bits of logic he still possessed.

As if his clothes burned his skin, he tore them off, tossing them onto the floor. Anita's eyes darkened as she scanned him. She looked at his erection, gasped, and met his gaze.

"You are even more beautiful than I imagined," she whispered.

He laughed softly. "That's my line, sweetheart."

He leaned over the bed to undress her, taking his time, enjoying every sweet morsel of her flesh as if she were a scrumptious dessert set out just for him.

He tugged off her boots, then her socks, and massaged her slim feet until she groaned. He slid her jeans down her hips and legs, flinging them next to his on the floor. She lifted her arms, allowing him to pull off her sweater.

He straightened to worship her with his eyes. Her thick black hair spread over the pillow, just as he'd dreamed. Her lush breasts strained against the white lace bra, and the matching panties barely covered her trimmed mound. She was a goddess, come to Earth, his goddess, all his for tonight. He wouldn't think beyond this moment.

Desire rushed at a fevered pace through him. He sank onto the bed next to her and gathered her into his arms. He savored the feel of her soft, hot skin. His throbbing cock pressed against her, wanting entry.

Not yet. First, he needed to taste every delicious inch of her.

He gently pushed her down onto the bed and kissed her with a hunger he'd never known with anyone before. She came alive in his arms. Her lips met his in a ravenous kiss, and she gripped his shoulders, digging her fingers into his flesh. Their tongues mated and explored each other in a primal duel.

He trailed kisses down her soft, white throat, nibbling the hot skin as he went. Her low moans fired his blood and sent heat, like sizzling oil, flowing through his veins.

He sat back and reached behind her to unhook her bra, releasing her full, round breasts. Stroking their fullness, he buried his head between them, inhaling her scent of arousal and warm musk.

He took one hard nipple into his mouth, sucking and licking. Her taste seared into his mind, enveloping him in her heat, and claiming a little bit more of his heart. He feasted on one breast, then the other, lost in her, needing her as he'd never needed anyone before. Uttering tiny cries, she threaded her fingers through his hair.

He moved slowly down her body, teasing her into submission, reveling in the softness of her pliant flesh. His mouth followed where his hands stroked. He kissed and nipped her flat belly, then removed her panties until she was gloriously naked, spread before him like a luscious feast. His cock throbbed so hard he was afraid he'd climax before he took her.

She was magnificent, beautiful, giving. Her seductive mix of strength and softness tore loose more of the barriers around his heart. He wanted to sink into her, to never let her go. The trust in her eyes spoke to a need deep inside him, urging him to let go of his past, of his fears, his guilt, and open himself to love.

Wanting to absorb all of her, he stroked her firm thighs, bent to kiss her mound. She writhed under him and whispered his name, immersing herself further into his very soul. He slid a finger into her hot folds, then another. As he continued his exploration, he watched the play of emotions on her face, the astonished pleasure, the need that glinted in her eyes. Selfishly, he wanted her all to himself, to wipe out any memories of other men, to would make her wholly and completely his and his alone. Her eyes widened, the wonder in them filling him with male pride. She stilled, then let out a scream as she climaxed in waves, over and over.

When her trembling body settled, Luke gathered her into his arms and kissed her temples and the corners of her mouth. He could stay like this forever, holding her, loving her.

Aching with his need for her, he slid off the bed to retrieve his jeans. Fishing in the pocket, he drew out a packet, opened it, and slipped on protection. He rejoined her on the bed, settling himself between her legs.

She touched his face and skimmed her fingers over his cheekbones to his lips. The softness and awe in her eyes brought light to the darkest places in his soul.

He sank into her, slowly at first, pushing in and pulling out, prolonging the ultimate pleasure. He couldn't wait any longer. With a low groan, he drove into her softness. She wrapped her legs around his hips and matched his rhythm, her eyes never leaving his. He drove harder and harder, losing himself in her, a starving man ravenous for what she offered. Her fingers dug into his shoulders as she arched her back, her hips pounding against his, her movements and her low cries urging him to go deeper.

With a cry of ecstasy, she climaxed again. His own climax quickly followed, and he growled her name. When their breathing slowed, he rolled off her, taking her with him.

She collapsed on top of him. "Luke."

The way she said his name, raw and filled with need, arrowed straight to his heart. When this mission was over, how on Earth could he give her up?

◇◇◇

Anita looked down at him. Her hair fell forward, touching his face. His beautiful face with his chocolate eyes, his high cheekbones, flushed from their lovemaking, his sensual lips that knew her body, knew how to work magic. Her heart felt ready to explode with happiness. She'd willingly given her body and soul to Luke. The fear she'd expected wasn't there, only satiation, a sense of belonging she hadn't felt in many years. If only they could stay like this forever, in their private cocoon holding the rest of the world at bay. But life didn't work that way.

She stroked his face with her fingers, wanting to prolong their time together.

He took her fingers into his mouth, one at a time, and sucked, eliciting a pleasure-filled sigh from her. Brushing his knuckles against her cheek, he whispered, "I think you've put a spell on me."

"No spell. I'm just an appreciative woman." But it was more than that. Since the first day she'd met Luke, she hadn't been able to get him out of her mind. Sure, he was hot as hell, but he made her feel alive, vibrant, protected. Mingled with the wildness she sensed in him, there was something innately good about him. When he touched her, held her, made love with her, she could almost feel her heart healing.

He pulled her against him. She buried her face in his neck. "What are you thinking?" he asked.

"About you and what we just did." She would keep her growing feelings for him tucked away to protect herself for the inevitable day when she and Luke parted.

He laughed. "We're not finished yet. So don't get too comfortable."

"Is that a promise?"

"Sure is, sweetheart."

With a soft laugh, she rolled off him and propped herself on her elbow facing him. For the first time, she noticed the tattoo on his right bicep. Reaching over, she traced her finger along the tat, a cross with a dagger through it. "What does this mean?"

A shadow flitted across his eyes. "I've had it a long time. It doesn't have any special meaning."

She didn't believe him. The part of her heart that had begun to open for him, closed.

Yet, she suspected the truth about the tattoo was something painful. She hoped someday he'd trust her enough to tell her.

Anita shivered with the cold. "I guess we'd better put the covers on."

They rolled down the comforter and sheets and slipped beneath them. She pulled the bedclothes around her neck and snuggled close to him.

Wanting him again, she rubbed her hand down his arms to his stomach, then lower. She wrapped her hand around his hard arousal. His penis jerked against her fingers. He was ready for her again. "Make love to me," she whispered.

Afterwards, as they lay in each other's arms, Luke's even breathing told her he slept soundly. She needed to sleep, too, but she couldn't. Luke had awakened something in her, a yearning she'd suppressed for years. And something she'd thought she'd lost—hope.

Her mind tumbled back to the scared, insecure sixteen-year-old she'd been when she lost her virginity to a classmate. Her parents had been killed the year before. Despite her close-knit, loving, extended family, her parents' deaths had left a tear in her soul.

Desperately wanting love and someone to belong to, she'd believed the guy when he said he loved her, that he'd take care of her. She willingly gave herself to him. Once he'd had her, he'd dumped her.

Although she thought she'd learned her lesson, she'd allowed herself to fall in love with Kent. And look where that had gotten her. Since Kent, there were men she'd dated whom she'd liked very much, good men, but when they got too close, she walked. It was what she did—enjoy a guy's company, enjoy him in bed, but never let him into her heart.

Fear raced through her now as she listened to Luke's steady breathing. He was an amazing lover, the best she'd had. But it was so much more than that. Unlike the others, she couldn't easily let him go.

Luke Corrado was a dangerous man.

CHAPTER THIRTEEN

The sluggish Delaware River was murky black in the predawn. Luke signaled for the men to follow more closely. Up ahead he could see shipping containers set out on the docks, waiting to be loaded onto trucks and transported across the country. The Port of Wilmington, Delaware, was ghost-quiet, the only sounds the rustling of rats and other night creatures in the swampy grasses. Things were too quiet. The hairs on the back of Luke's neck stood at attention.

Massive cargo ships rocked gently in the water, gigantic sentinels keeping watch over the darkness. In a few hours, the place would be bustling with activity as trucks arrived and departed and more containers were unloaded from the ships. The container Luke and his men sought would be moved out before the others. There wasn't much time.

When the tip came in to the Philly field office, and no time to call in reinforcements from Baltimore, Luke had convinced Murray to let him head this detail. Sitting behind a desk all day grated on his nerves and he needed an outlet. Now, riding high on adrenaline, the scent of danger all around, Luke reveled in the excitement. He was never more alive than when he was on a dangerous job.

As soon as the thought was out, he knew it was no longer true. Anita had changed everything. His soul had come alive again when they'd made love two days ago.

A rustle in the bushes snapped him back to the mission. His instincts kicked in. Something felt wrong. Luke gripped his Glock tighter. The ski mask he wore itched, but it was necessary.

86

If they ran into any members of the human trafficking gang, he had to keep his identity secret. He didn't trust this unknown person who'd phoned in the tip. According to the tipster's call late last night, the human cargo was due to be moved at dawn. The Agency had to act fast.

As backup, a SWAT team from the local police ringed the perimeter of the dock as Luke and his band of five special agents walked stealthily toward the container they hunted. Distinguished from the others, it was marked with a red slash across the back, exactly as they'd been told. When Luke reached it, he signaled again. Baranov, one of his men, strode up carrying a chain cutter. He clipped the lock on the chain strung across the double doors.

His senses on high alert, unsure of what he'd find, but prepared to shoot, Luke, with Baranov's help, opened the heavy steel doors. They stepped aside, then, cautiously, Baranov shined his flashlight into the interior.

Bile rose in Luke's throat. No matter how many times he'd confronted evidence of man's inhumanity to man, the sight before him made him want to retch. Terrified faces of young women and children, huddled together and shivering in the cold, looked out at them.

Gun drawn, Baranov cautiously stepped forward and said something in rapid Russian to the terror-stricken people staring back. One of the women answered, her high-pitched voice shaking.

"Same story as always." Baranov turned to Luke. "They were promised jobs in America. They've been traveling for weeks now, with very little food or water. A few of the kids are sick."

"Fucking monsters who did this," Luke spat out. "Call Murray. Let him know."

Luke gripped the sides of the container and climbed in. The other men with him started forward. The SWAT team appeared from the shadows.

Just as Baranov took out his phone to call Murray, shots rang out. Baranov went down in a heap.

Luke jumped from the container, crouched on the ground, and aimed his gun toward the bushes, where the gunfire had come from. More shots rang out. The agents and the SWAT team went into action. The entire port erupted with the sounds of gunfire and flashes of light from the automatic weapons. Finally, all was quiet.

Luke stayed close to the container, using it as a shield, and did a quick assessment of the area. With the exception of Baranov, none of his men or members of the SWAT team had fallen.

The SWAT team, guns ready, explored the nearby swamp grasses. Luke's men fanned out to search the area closest to the container. Luke bent over Baranov, relieved to see he'd suffered only a shoulder wound.

Screams and cries came from the container. Luke held up a hand, trying to silence the frightened occupants and convey to them everything would be okay. He was sure his wearing a ski mask didn't do much to comfort them.

"Hang in there, buddy," Luke said to Baranov. "You'll be okay."

Luke punched in the phone code for Murray. "We need an ambulance," he said when Murray answered. "Had a little fire fight. Baranov's been hit, but it doesn't look serious."

"I'll get one over there right away," Murray said. "Did you get the cargo?"

"Yeah."

"Over here!" one of the SWAT team called out. "We got one of the shooters."

"Got one of the shooters. Call you later." Luke disconnected the call and ran toward the edge of the bushes where a group of SWAT members stood looking down at a body.

◇◇◇

"What the fuck happened out there?" Murray rubbed a hand over his bald pate and paced his office.

"A setup?" Luke suggested. Too tense to sit, he stood in front of Murray's desk. "Who was this informant who dropped the dime about the cargo? How do we know he wasn't setting us up?"

Murray stopped pacing and sat on the edge of the desk. His bulging stomach hung over the waistband of his pants. "Why would they sacrifice a valuable cargo just to take down a few Feds? What are we missing? We don't know who gave us the info. The agent who took the message said the caller disguised his voice. Maybe he has a grudge against the gang." He chuckled. "A disgruntled employee."

"If it wasn't a trap, the shooters were there to move the cargo." Luke strode to the window and turned to face Murray. "Guess they were shocked to see us. Good thing we got there in time." He pounded a fist against his thigh as the faces of those terrified women and children swam before him. They were in federal protective custody now. All had been examined by medical personnel, and a few had been admitted to the hospital, under police guard. The Agency hoped some of the women had information that could help the authorities find the leaders of the criminal gang.

"We have to get those monsters doing this," Luke said, his voice tight. "We've been tracking them for five years and we're not any closer than when we started."

Murray grabbed a pencil off his desk, broke it in half, threw the pieces onto the floor. "Damn bastards. We can't get discouraged. We have to believe we're making a difference. In a perfect world no one would prey on children and the innocent, but that's never gonna happen. We've put away a lot of criminals and rescued hundreds of kids and women from lives of horror. Give yourself some credit for that."

Murray settled on the desk and rested a hand on his belly. "Once we ID the guy killed, we might be able to trace his movements and his contacts, maybe find who hired him."

Blood pounded in Luke's ears. "How many more women and children will be killed or sold into the sex trade before we crack this case? Are you sure our intel is legit, about the leader being in Philly?"

"Our sources are good. The bastard is here. We'll get him."

Murray furrowed his brow. "How are things going with the Santisi woman? Any idea what Sweeney did with that list?"

Guilt made Luke glance away for a few seconds. Making love with Anita wasn't part of his job. But he didn't regret the other night. When this job was over and he was assigned somewhere else, would he break her heart? He didn't want to hurt her, but at least she understood the game. Anita wasn't looking for happy-ever-after. Still, the thought of hurting her in any way felt like a dagger to his heart.

"Corrado?"

He met his supervisor's gaze. "If I'd found anything new I would have told you."

"Maybe we're wrong to pursue that lead."

"The gang thinks she has it or they wouldn't be going after her. Sweeney must have said something to them before he died. If they're after Anita, there's a good reason. I'll find that list."

"Don't let me down this time," Murray said.

"You can count on me."

◇◇◇

"Jo, we'll make an Italian of you yet," Anita said. "This wedding soup is wonderful."

Anita, Jo, Aunt Lena and Nonna sat around Nonna's highly polished mahogany dining room table in her tiny South Philadelphia row house eating the Italian wedding soup they'd made earlier. Making the soup near the holidays was a Santisi family tradition. The comforting hominess—the fifty-year-old flowered wallpaper on the dining room walls, the pictures of Nonna's children, grandchildren and great-grandchildren that covered the doily-topped mahogany server—made Anita's heart overflow with love for her family.

"I enjoy making the soup and I had good teachers," Jo said. "And I've always liked cooking." She laughed. "That was one of my well-kept secrets until I married Franco. It didn't go with my tough-girl image." Her cheeks pinked. "And I want to do everything I can to make him happy. He's pleased when I spend time with his family."

Aunt Lena reached over and placed her hand over her daughter-in-law's. "Jo, you're the best thing to ever happen to my son. We're so glad to have you in our family."

Jo smiled, and Anita caught a glisten of tears in her eyes. "Thanks, Mom," Jo said. "I'm lucky to have all of you."

Anita broke some of the crusty bread they served with the soup and rolled her eyes. "Okay, enough of the mushy stuff. Let's enjoy this soup."

Her grandmother's brown eyes, clouded with age, studied Anita. "You'll find your special man, too, Anita."

Aunt Lena put down her spoon. "Yes, it's your turn now. We want you to find someone too."

Anita shrugged. "You know me. I don't need a man, at least not permanently." It had been two days since she and Luke made love, yet the memory of his lips and hands, the way he held her, the way his body moved over hers, his whispered words, were never far from her mind. She picked up her wine glass and sipped, trying to dissolve the heat swirling through her at the memories.

Jo chuckled and gave Anita a teasing look. "Speaking of men, what's going on with you and your new neighbor? You two looked pretty friendly the night of the Cutfords' Christmas party."

"What neighbor?" Aunt Lena asked. "Who is he?"

"He's my neighbor. Nothing more." Anita shot Jo a narrow-eyed look. Jo laughed and went back to eating her soup.

"Tell us about him," Nonna said.

Aunt Lena and Nonna were on a mission to get all Nonna's grandchildren married. Now that Doriana was settled and happy with Logan, Jo and Franco were vying for "couple of the year" in their happiness, and Anita's other cousins were all married and producing babies, Nonna and Aunt Lena had set their formidable matchmaking skills on Anita.

"What's his name? What does he do?" Aunt Lena asked.

With a sigh, Anita set down her wine glass. She couldn't fight Nonna and Aunt Lena when they ganged up on her. "His name is Luke Corrado. He founded a software company, sold it, and now he consults with other software companies. He's subletting the loft next to mine while he's in Philly doing some consulting work."

"Where is he from?" Aunt Lena asked.

"Tucson."

"Really? I wonder if Logan knows him."

Anita ate more soup before answering. "Tucson is a big place. Logan can't know everyone who lives there."

"Your new neighbor has no family nearby?" Nonna asked.

"I don't think so. He doesn't talk about family." Anxiety sat like a hunk of stale bread in Anita's chest. She knew what was coming. She'd thought of bringing Luke to her family's annual Christmas Eve party but now wasn't sure. He was a fling to her, no different from the other men she'd dated since Kent. *Yeah, right.*

"You must invite him to our Christmas party," Aunt Lena said right on cue, a self-satisfied smile on her face.

"Yes, invite him," Jo agreed.

Anita shot Jo a look. Jo was having way too much fun.

"I don't know him well enough to invite him to our Christmas party. He's only a friend." *And a lover.* "I don't want him to get any ideas. You know I'm not into commitment."

"Nonsense," Nonna said. "We're not a family that turns anyone away at Christmas. If he has no family nearby, we must make him feel welcome."

Aunt Lena looked at Anita with soft brown eyes. "You keep saying you're commitment-phobic, but I think you're trying to convince yourself. Kent happened a long time ago, dear. You need to let it go."

Anita bristled. "I have let it go."

But she hadn't. Her family didn't know the full story of what Kent had done to her. And she couldn't admit to them the emotional damage Kent's betrayal had inflicted.

"Your friend will come to our party," Aunt Lena said in her *my word is authority* voice. The subject closed, she tackled her soup.

CHAPTER FOURTEEN

When he heard a car door slam outside, Luke raced to the window and looked out onto the street fronting his place. With a relieved sigh, he saw Anita lock her car and hurry up the steps. He knew one of the cars parked down the street belonged to Jo and Harris's security team.

Once the Agency got the list and began the crackdown on the human trafficking group, he could leave for his next assignment convinced Anita would be out of harm's way. But, right now, she needed his protection. And he needed to see her, touch her, hold her. He didn't question why he felt that way, only that he'd missed her the last two days.

Fifteen minutes later, he knocked on her door. He saw her look through the peephole before the dead bolt turned. She stepped aside to let him in, then re-engaged her security alarm.

In tight faded jeans, a brown long-sleeved T-shirt, her feet bare, and her long black hair streaming down her back, he wanted to scoop her into his arms and carry her to that king-size bed.

"You're wearing something other than black again," he said, letting his gaze scan her sexy body. "You look great."

Laughing, she moved into the condo, and he followed. "Thanks. I was at my grandmother's today making Italian wedding soup with her, my aunt and Jo. I had to wear something I didn't mind dirtying."

She headed toward the bar set up in a corner of the living area. "Want a drink?"

"Sure." Catching up to her, he grabbed her around the waist and turned her to face him. "But a drink can wait. I want you." He brushed strands of her hair back from her face. "I've missed you."

Her large eyes lit with something hot and needy. His body stirred in response.

"I've missed you, too." She wound her arms around his neck and kissed him.

His appetite for her couldn't be satiated. He needed her again. And again. Maybe he'd finally get his fill of her. He doubted it.

With a small moan, she opened her mouth to his invasion. She tasted like wine and Italian spices. He wanted to devour her.

He backed her up against the wall. "Now, Anita."

"Yes."

They quickly shed their clothes and he pulled on protection. He backed her against the wall again and cradled her butt, lifting her. She wrapped her legs around his waist. He thrust deeply into her, eliciting moans of pleasure from her. They climaxed together, their cries filling the room.

◇◇◇

Later, they sat on the sofa in front of a snapping fire, drinking wine and eating Italian wedding soup Anita had brought home. She felt warm and happy, happier than she'd been in a long time. And satisfied. Very satisfied. She had to be careful her feelings for Luke didn't get out of control. *Little too late for that.*

He set his empty bowl on the coffee table and placed his arm around her shoulders drawing her close. "Soup is delicious. But not as delicious as you." He brushed a feather-soft kiss on her temple.

She set down her own bowl and settled against him. For a while, she would forget her home was a fortress and that someone might be trying to kill her. She turned in Luke's arms and ran her fingers up his chest to his face. When he smiled, she swirled the tip of her finger around his dimple. "I like your dimple."

He laughed. "It's there just for you."

"I'll bet you say that to all the girls."

His features tensed. "Not for a long time."

"Did someone hurt you?"

He looked at her with hooded eyes. "No one hurt me." He glanced away. "But I've hurt others."

She started to ask who he'd hurt, but clamped her mouth shut. A part of her yearned to know every facet of Luke Corrado, what made him tick, his likes and dislikes, to know about his childhood, his needs and wants. But he closed off so much of himself, she suspected he wouldn't tell her what she needed to know. She told herself that was for the best, but she couldn't stop the little twinge of regret that she'd never find the real man behind the sexy, charming, warm façade.

Forcing her unhappy thoughts away, Anita kissed him lightly on the lips and settled herself more comfortably against him. With a sigh, she said, "Christmas is in ten days."

"Is it? I haven't been paying attention."

She pulled away and looked at him. "How could you not pay attention? Christmas is all around us. Carols playing on every radio station. Decorations. Frantic shoppers." She tapped his forehead. "Earth to Luke. Where have you been?"

He shrugged and reached for the glass of wine he'd set down. The flames from the fire reflected in the deep burgundy of the alcohol, the rich colors of Christmas, a Christmas Luke didn't seem to care about.

He stared into the wine so long she thought he wouldn't answer. Finally, he took a long sip, and holding the glass between his hands, he shifted his attention to the fire, not looking at her. "Christmas doesn't mean much to me any more."

"That's very sad."

"I'm good with it."

"You don't have plans for Christmas Eve and Christmas Day?"

"No, but in the past I've volunteered at a soup kitchen. It gives me something to do."

"My cousin Doriana's husband, Logan, used to do that. He lives in Tucson."

Luke stiffened, set down his glass, turned to her. "Tucson? I wonder if I know him."

"His name is Logan Tanner and he owns a security firm specializing in corporate espionage. He helped Uncle Dan's company, Franco's now, six years ago."

Luke appeared lost in thought. Finally, his features relaxed and he shook his head. "I don't know him."

"Would you like to meet him?" she blurted.

"What?"

She'd gone and done it now. She'd have to ask him to the family Christmas party. Luke needed to be with loving people for the holidays to help take away the sadness she sensed in him. But there was another reason she asked—so she could be with *him*.

"My family hosts a huge party every Christmas Eve," she said. "It's a tradition around here. It's at Jo and Franco's this year. I'd like you to come."

He studied her for long minutes with unreadable eyes, making her squirm, sure he'd say no.

Finally, he gave her another of his dimpled smiles. "I'd like to come with you. Thanks for asking." He bent his head and kissed her, his mouth soft yet firm. They slid down onto the sofa together.

◇◇◇

Hours later, alone and back at his place, Luke lay on his bed, too keyed up to sleep. A thrill wound through him thinking about Anita and their lovemaking. She was passionate, responsive, and willing to do anything he wanted. And she wasn't afraid to take the lead. He smiled. In all ways, she was one hell of a woman.

His smile faded. She'd gotten to him, to that part of him he'd thought dead. When he was with her, he felt complete in a way he never had before. But he and Anita had no future. He wasn't a forever kind of guy, not since Maria. And he liked it that way. He suspected for all Anita's independence and strength, deep inside she needed someone who would love her and be by her side always. He wasn't that guy.

His private cell phone rang and he jumped up. His heart pounded when he saw the number that came up. Maria's!

"Who the hell is this?" he said in Spanish when he connected the call. "What game are you playing?"

"Mr. Luis, I am sorry. No games." The same hesitant female voice from the other calls responded in Spanish.

"Adelina?" He held the phone in a death grip.

"Yes, I am Adelina."

Maria's chaperone, the elderly woman her brother had hired to keep Maria "pure." Lot of good that had done. Adelina had liked him and encouraged his relationship with her charge.

"Adelina, what do you want? Are you okay?"

"Oh, Mr. Luis, I cannot hide your son much longer. Mr. Mendoza knows about little Miguel. He has men looking for him. They will kill him."

Luke felt as if the blood flowing through his veins had turned to ice. A rushing noise filled his head. He sank onto the bed. "What are you talking about? I have no son."

"After you left Mexico the first time, Maria had your son. She was scared of her brother, so I took Miguel to hide him. When her brother found out about the baby, she told him it died at birth. Now he knows she lied. My cousin, he hears things. He said word is that Mendoza will kill Miguel. Mendoza calls Miguel gringo bastard that doesn't deserve to live."

"I have a son?" Luke's brain shut down. He couldn't have heard right. Why hadn't Maria told him she was pregnant? "How old is my—he?"

"Miguel is a little over two years."

"Why didn't you contact me before this?"

"I was afraid. When you came back for Maria, she was so happy. She was going to come get Miguel and the three of you would go to the United States." Adelina sobbed. "But Mendoza killed her. After that, I was too scared to call you or to leave here. If I tried to reach you, Mr. Mendoza might know where I was. But now the relatives I live with tell me I have to go because Mr. Mendoza has people looking for me, and they are close."

Luke stood. His mind cleared. "Where are you, Adelina?"

She named a small town deep in the mountains outside

Mexico City. The place was a haven for drug dealers and smugglers.

"Why did you go there? It's dangerous."

"I have family. No one bothered us, until now."

Skepticism reared up in Luke. It could be a trap. But he'd known Adelina to be honest and intensely loyal to Maria. Besides, if that really was the child's age, the timing was right.

"I'll get you both out of there, Adelina."

CHAPTER FIFTEEN

"In the name of all that's holy, you are not going into Mexico. Did you forget there's a bounty on your head?" Murray slammed his fist on his desk, sending papers flying.

After Adelina's phone call last night, Luke hadn't slept much and had gotten to the field office before Murray arrived for work. Murray found him pacing in front of his office.

Luke leaned over the desk until they were nose to nose. "It's my son. I have to go. I can't leave him to Mendoza. I don't give a damn about the price on my head."

"Well, you'd give a damn if you were killed and your son along with you. Calm down, Corrado, and think about this rationally." Murray's eyes softened. "How can you be sure he's your son or if there's even a child? It could all be a scam to get you back there."

"Adelina is honest and she was devoted to Maria." Luke straightened and smoothed a hand over his hair. "I can't be one hundred percent sure, but the timing is right, and Maria and I loved each other. I believe he's my son." He grimaced. "If I do nothing, and it turns out he is my son and Mendoza kills him…" Trying to gain control over his roiling emotions, he glanced away.

"You have a job here," Murray said. "You can't go flying off to Mexico to what might be a con to lure you back. Mendoza has had a hard-on for you since he found out you were a Fed and fooling around with his sister."

Luke turned back to Murray. "If Adelina's telling the truth, I can't leave the child and her in danger."

"Settle down. Let me make a few calls. We have some nationals working in the area." Murray gave him an understanding smile. "Maybe they can find out if this woman and child are there. If so, we'll try to rescue them. You understand we can't jeopardize our people or the mission."

"I understand but I refuse to accept it."

Murray waved a hand, silencing Luke. "We'll do everything we can. Trust me. You get that damn list."

◇◇◇

That evening, hands stuffed in his jacket pockets and his collar pulled up against the December wind blowing between the high buildings, Luke strode along Chestnut Street. He'd needed to walk to clear his mind of his conflicting emotions—pain for the suffering of the victims of the trafficking gang, frustration that they hadn't found the group's leader, his worry over Anita's safety, and his fear for his son. If Miguel was his son. Luke had accepted Adelina's story, and knew in his heart the child was his and Maria's, yet part of him remained cautious.

Dismissing his troubling thoughts, he tried to focus on his surroundings. Christmas decorations adorned the upscale shops, and twinkling multi-colored lights were strung across the street. On one corner, carolers sang Christmas songs while passersby tossed coins for the needy into the bucket. Luke threw in a twenty dollar bill as he went past. Well-dressed shoppers of every age, most holding large bags, hurried by, their faces strained and intent. Worried about getting all their shopping done before Christmas, he figured.

Christmas! *Bah Humbug*! Luke felt like Scrooge. He hadn't celebrated Christmas in years, didn't know if he believed in God anymore, not after the suffering and violence he'd seen. Not since his sister Sofia died. And Maria.

He had a son, someone who would depend on him, someone else to keep safe. And he would give his life to protect him. Murray would do everything in his power to rescue the boy, but Luke knew the Agency wouldn't put their agents in harm's way. The undercover work they did in Mexico was too important.

Luke wanted desperately to go to Mexico, guns blazing like

a cowboy in an old Western. But Murray was right. A dead Luke couldn't help his son.

After his talk with Murray this morning, he'd spent the day at the field office interrogating some of the poor souls they'd rescued from the cargo container. The women and children were traumatized by their ordeal, making it difficult to get much information from them. The language barrier didn't help, even with the Russian translator there.

From what the victims said, they'd been promised jobs in America, along with visas, and in some cases, new identities. Some of the children belonged to the women who'd been held captive. But other children appeared to have been kidnapped. They were the ones Luke felt the most sorry for. He hoped the Agency could find their parents.

Each woman told the same story—she'd met a good-looking, well-dressed man who showered her with compliments and gifts and took her nice places. After a whirlwind romance of a few days, the man would tell the woman he could get her a job in America, and he would handle all the paperwork she'd need. The women jumped at the chance to leave their hardscrabble lives for a better one.

They'd been driven to the docks and thrown into the cargo containers. Fed once a day and given buckets for their bathroom needs, they'd endured cold, inhumane conditions.

As he strode down the street, Luke shoved his hands deeper into his pockets, fighting the surge of anger that heated him despite the cold. The women and children they'd rescued were the lucky ones. He'd seen what happened to the unlucky wretches. The women would be distributed to brothels all over the world. Living in cramped rooms, given drugs until they were addicts, forced to perform sex acts, their souls crushed. Dependency on drugs kept them from running away. The armed brutes guarding the brothels kept them in line too, with beatings and rapes.

Luke walked faster. His breath hovered in the cold air. The children were the saddest of all. Sold into slavery to pedophiles, they were sexually abused until they got too old for the perverts who owned them. Then they were killed, their bodies dumped in alleyways and dumpsters, like garbage. He'd seen enough to make him sick, to make him believe there couldn't be a God. What just God would allow such depravity?

Someone on the sidewalk jostled Luke, tearing him from his dark musings. A pretty young woman smiled an apology. Interest lit her eyes as she scanned him. She gave him a flirty smile. A few well-chosen words would convince the woman to have a drink with him, to maybe come home with him.

He returned her smile and kept walking. The only woman he wanted was Anita. Thinking about her made his body tighten with need. Just hearing her voice or seeing her smile made him happy in a way he hadn't been in years. With her in his life, he could envision a future filled with love and peace.

He had too much old baggage. Anita deserved better.

Forcing his thoughts from Anita, he found himself on the lower end of Chestnut. Sweeney's antique shop was a few streets over. The FBI had torn the place apart looking for the list. The Agency found nothing to pinpoint that Sweeney had knowledge of the crime gang's dealings or who the leader was.

A sense of urgency or curiosity, he didn't know which, propelled Luke to walk faster and head for the antique shop. Standing in front of the closed and darkened store, he peered through the dirty plate glass. The shop had been shuttered before the police found Sweeney's body. According to the employees, Sweeney had texted he'd found a buyer for the place and wanted it closed immediately. Since the text had come from Sweeney's phone, the police hadn't been able to trace who'd sent it. Luke closed his eyes against the regret and sadness that pounded him. Poor Sweeney.

Opening his eyes, Luke stared through the window, then froze. A small beam of light danced against the wall in the back of the store. What the hell? Thieves? Or someone from the cartel looking for the list?

He hid in the shadow of the doorway and called Murray. When his supervisor answered, Luke hurriedly explained and hung up before Murray could order him to stand down. Hell, no!

He was going in.

Using the small burglar's pick he carried, Luke worked the door's lock until it swung open. If there was a security alarm, it was a silent one. He hoped it was still operational. Gun in hand, he crept slowly toward the light, careful not to make noise. The old wooden floorboards squeaked in protest, and he scrunched against the wall, listening. Nothing indicated that whoever was here had heard the sound.

Hugging the walls, he headed to the spot he'd last seen the beam. The shop was small, but an open door separated it from a large storage area in the back. Gripping his Glock, prepared to fire, he slipped through the door into the larger room.

He heard a shuffling to his right and turned as someone leaped toward him. Luke fired and his attacker went down. A shot rang out, just missing him. Luke took cover behind some boxes. When the boxes across from him fell, he knew the other shooter was hiding behind them. The guy poked his head up to fire at Luke. Luke ducked, jumped up and fired back.

More shots, followed by the sound of a gun jamming. The hairs on the back of Luke's neck stood in warning and he whirled around. Too late. A third perp had sneaked up behind him. Before Luke could fire, the man pounced, knocking Luke to the ground. Luke's gun flew out of his hands. The ruffian pinned Luke and hit him hard on the jaw, then his nose. He felt the warm trickle of blood on his face.

Anger surged through Luke, giving him renewed strength. He kicked the brute in the groin, then pushed up from the floor. The man tried to sidle away, but Luke tackled him. On top now, Luke punched him over and over. These could be ordinary burglars, but something told Luke they were more than that. Another guy jumped on Luke's back and wrapped his arm around Luke's neck, pressing against his windpipe.

"Police! Drop your weapons." Someone pulled the guy off him. Luke staggered and gasped for air.

The cops handcuffed the perp Luke had been throttling and pulled him to his feet. They'd handcuffed the other guy and shoved him against the wall.

Murray entered and handed Luke a handkerchief. Luke held it to his nose.

"I shot one," Luke said, his voice barely audible.

"We got him," Murray said.

Around them, agents and police secured the area. Paramedics rushed in and put the thug Luke had shot onto a stretcher. The scumbag groaned, and Luke was almost sorry he hadn't killed the bastard.

"I wanted to kill those sonsofbitches," Luke muttered, taking the handkerchief from his nose.

"I know," Murray said. "We need these jerks alive, Corrado." He studied Luke and smiled. "Hope your nose isn't broken. It'd be a shame to mess up that pretty face."

"Stuff it, Murray."

Murray laughed. "Let's get one of the paramedics to look at it."

After the EMT team treated him and assured Luke his nose wasn't broken, he refused Murray's offer of a ride home. He needed to walk off his rage. Damn it! He'd wanted to pommel those guys, wanted to make them suffer the way they'd made the innocents suffer.

And he wanted his son, here with him, safe and sound.

What a fucking frustrating nightmare.

CHAPTER SIXTEEN

He felt like hell. Luke reclined on his sectional, an ice pack to his nose. The nose might not be broken, but it sure hurt. He had the beginnings of a bruise on his jaw, and his leg ached. He must have hurt it when the thug knocked him down. Home for an hour, he'd had a beer and a piece of cold leftover pizza. He didn't have much of an appetite.

Murray had called with an update. The guy Luke had shot was in surgery, with police protection. The others had been treated for minor wounds and were in a holding cell at police headquarters. The scums could rot in hell for all Luke cared. The Agency would question all three men, but he doubted they'd get much. That kind of scumbag was usually more afraid of whoever they worked for than they were of the police or the FBI.

A knock at his door had Luke grabbing for the gun that lay on the table in front of him. He put down the ice pack, pushed up from the sectional, and trod cautiously to the door. When he looked through the peephole and saw Anita, relief and pleasure washed over him.

"Just a minute," he shouted through the door. He jammed his gun into the back waistband of his jeans and covered it with his shirt. He couldn't wear the gun when he was with her, and he couldn't let her see it.

"My God, you look awful," she said when he opened the door. "Were you in a fight?"

"Something like that. I was mugged, but I fought him off." He tried to smile. "You should see the other guy." Despite the necessity of lying to her, guilt stuck in his gut like a knife.

"That's terrible." She took his arm and led him to the sectional. "You need to rest. Stay right here. I've got some wedding soup left. I'll get it and be right back."

"No. I don't want you going out there, just in case. You took a chance coming here."

She rolled her eyes. "I'm only next door."

"I'm still worried about you going out more than you have to. I've got canned soup here, but I'm not hungry."

"You need to eat. Canned soup can't compare to Nonna's, but it'll do. You rest and I'll take care of you."

"I appreciate it but I can take care of myself."

"Damn stubborn man. Don't argue."

He sank onto the seat and held up his hands in resignation. "I know better than to argue with a determined woman."

She smiled. "You remember that, mister."

"What are you doing here anyway? Not that I'm objecting."

"You were limping a little on your way in. I was worried about you."

His throat thickened. No one had worried about him for a very long time. Being with Anita could be addictive.

While she fixed the soup, he hid his gun in the drawer of one of the side tables.

Fifteen minutes later, she had two steaming bowls of chicken soup and warm crusty rolls set up in the small dining area. Insisting he could walk to the table by himself, Luke refused her offer to help. The woman was hell-bent on babying him. If he was honest with himself he'd admit he liked it. He shrugged away the thought.

Luke sat at the table and inhaled the comforting aroma of chicken soup. "You're going to spoil me," he said with a smile.

The sweet smile she returned sent warmth through him that rivaled the heat of the soup.

"So long as you don't spoil me, we're good," she said.

He broke off a piece of the hot roll, slathered butter on it, and met her gaze. "Why shouldn't I spoil you?"

She lifted her chin. "I don't need spoiling, thank you very

much. I can take care of myself."

"I'd enjoy spoiling you, in many different ways." His voice had turned husky. He scanned her face, flushed from the hot soup. Or because of him? Her full lips parted, moist and inviting. Strands of her thick black hair trailed over her shoulders to touch the tips of her lush breasts under the tight black sweater. The need to kiss every square inch of her delicious body made his jeans tighten uncomfortably.

"Trust me, I neither need nor want spoiling." She grabbed a roll and broke off a piece. "Considering the lack of food in your refrigerator and pantry, I was surprised to find these rolls in the freezer." She shook her head. "I thought you liked to cook, but you have a typical bachelor refrigerator. Leftover pizza and beer."

"I do like to cook, but I haven't had much time for grocery shopping."

"I see you favor Mexican beer." She nodded toward the bottle in front of him. "You have plenty of that."

He took a spoonful of soup and a bite of roll, wincing at the sharp pain that shot through his nose when he chewed. He decided to ignore the remark about the beer. He didn't want to talk about Mexico in any way right now. He waved a piece of the roll in front of him. "I have a weakness for fresh bread. Got it at this little Italian bakery in South Philly."

She laughed. "It's good stuff. My grandmother lives in South Philly. She probably buys her bread at the same bakery."

He put down his spoon, leaned toward her across the table, and placed his hand over hers. His injuries forgotten, some need in him incited him to say, "Tell me about Anita Santisi. Have you always lived in Philly?"

"Born and bred. I wouldn't live anywhere else. What about you? You said you had a house in California, but sold it. So you have no permanent home?"

"I live wherever my work takes me." Not an outright lie. He didn't need to tell her about the sparsely furnished apartment he kept in Tucson. He pulled away and concentrated on finishing his soup. Tucson brought memories of the barrio, the poverty-ridden childhood, Sofia. He refused to let his mind go there.

Later, their drinks on the table in front of them, they sat on the sectional and watched TV. Or rather, Luke watched Anita while she watched TV. Her profile reminded him of Ancient Roman statues of noblewomen he'd seen in Rome.

"What?" she said turning to him.

He threw her a teasing smile. "Just enjoying looking at you. And picturing you walking around a villa in Ancient Rome."

"You must have taken a knock to the head," she said. "Or had too much beer."

"No knock to the head and I'm completely sober." He leaned closer. "Have you ever been to Rome?"

"A few times."

"You remind me of the noblewomen I saw in statues and paintings there."

She laughed. "Now I know you hurt your head. That is the strangest pickup line I've ever heard."

He brushed his knuckles over the creamy skin of her cheek. She pinked to a rosy glow. "I don't need a pickup line because you already know how much I want you, all the time."

She reached behind him and grabbed the ice pack. "Put this on and cool off. You need to rest."

"Yes, boss." He slid away and held the melting ice pack to his nose.

She sipped her drink and stared at the TV. He wondered if she actually saw what was on the screen.

"Anita."

Frowning, she turned to him. "Do you need something? More ice?"

I need you. Instead he said, "You're good at taking care of people. Why haven't you married and had kids?"

A shadow fell over her eyes, but disappeared so quickly he wondered if he'd imagined it. "First of all," she said. "If you tell anyone I took care of you, I will have to kill you. You'll ruin my reputation in the city and with my family."

"My lips are sealed."

"And, second, as for why I'm not married, I've never felt the need, except once, and that ended badly."

"What happened?"

"Now, you're pushing it." Her smile took the edge from her words. "Let's just say he wasn't who I thought he was."

Guilt squeezed Luke's chest. He wasn't who she thought he was either. "How long ago was that?"

Anita finished off her drink and stood. "I need more wine. Want another beer?"

"I'm good." Luke watched her walk into the kitchen. He scrubbed a hand over his face. She'd shut down. He had to stay away from that line of questioning in the future. But he needed her to feel comfortable confiding in him. Maybe she'd remember something about Sweeney that would give him a clue as to where the list was.

Who the hell was he fooling? He wanted her to feel comfortable with him for personal reasons too. He cared for her.

As she strode back toward him, full glass of wine in hand, he acknowledged the hurt that mingled with his frustration. Hurt she didn't care enough about him to confide. Frustration that she was still in danger.

She sat down and sipped the wine before turning to him. "Tell me more about you, Luke Corrado. Ever married?"

He sat straighter and dropped the ice pack onto the table. "I'm not married, have never been married."

"No children, then, I assume."

I have a son I've just learned about, whom I've never met. A son I'm determined to bring home.

He shook his head as if he could shake away the sadness that pulsed through him. He held out his arms to her. "Come here. I want to hold you."

She hesitated for a fraction of a second before she put her glass down and moved closer. He wrapped his arms around her and gathered her to him. He reclined sideways, making room for her. She squeezed close, chest-to-chest, and tucked her head under his chin.

"Your hair smells good," he said. "Grapefruit."

"I've started selling a new brand of hair care products. This is my favorite."

He kissed the top of her head. "Always the hard-working businesswoman."

"You could say that."

"I admire what you've done," he said. "But you've got too much love and caring in you to not share it with a husband and children. Do you want children?"

She stiffened and he was afraid she'd pull away, but she relaxed and settled more closely against him. "I thought I wanted kids once, but it's too late. I'm pushing forty."

"So am I. Forty isn't old, not anymore. You'd make a great mother."

"You don't know me that well."

"I know all I need to about you." He held her closer. "I like holding you." He laughed softly. "I like doing a lot more than that with you."

"Down, boy, not tonight. You've been hurt and my job is to take care of you."

Resting his chin on her head, he closed his eyes against the melancholy swirling through him. He could picture himself coming home to Anita every day, having her love him and care about his welfare. His son, too, was part of the homey picture of a life he'd long ago denied himself.

But he couldn't allow himself to dream. A family life filled with love died the day his father walked out. His mother had loved him and Sofia, but his father's abandonment had made her bitter, and she worked herself to death providing for her kids.

Luke inhaled Anita's sweet scent and willed away the dream. He'd chosen a different life.

CHAPTER SEVENTEEN

Luke locked his car and strode along Chestnut to Anita's salon. She'd invited him to her annual Christmas party for her staff and her best clients. A week before Christmas, and he wanted the holiday over. But he'd hidden his feelings, as he'd learned to do long ago.

He wanted his son here with him, too. Murray reported agents in Mexico had conducted surveillance on the site, and they'd confirmed an older woman and a small boy lived at the house. Word had reached them that Mendoza and his cronies were in the area asking about a woman and a young boy. Murray assured Luke it was only a matter of time before the agents could rescue them. Every cell in Luke's body thrummed with wanting to go to Mexico himself, to storm the house where his son was and take him home. Wherever home was.

Then his real work would begin. Hell, did he even know how to be a father? Growing up, he'd had no male role model.

As he walked, he rubbed his aching jaw, still hurting from the attack at Sweeney's shop days ago. The bruise had yellowed, but at least his nose was no longer swollen. He'd been right that the police and the Agency couldn't get anything out of the intruders. A dead end. The thugs insisted they were merely trying to rob the place. They had no priors, and Luke suspected they knew they'd get out on bail. The one he'd shot was still in the hospital, but the other ones had already made bail.

Thoughts of the attack brought Anita to his mind. She'd fussed over him, and he liked her fussing, maybe liked it a little too much.

111

She'd called every morning to see how he was feeling, and each night after she got home. Last night, he'd gone to her place and they'd made love. Not wanting to leave her, he'd stayed over. But she'd seemed uncomfortable this morning with him there and he figured she didn't have many men stay over. That thought pleased him more than it should have.

He reached her shop, which was brightly lit with small white lights around the large picture window. Steeling himself for a round of unwanted Christmas cheer, he opened the door and stepped inside.

Holiday music, scents of vanilla and cinnamon, laughter and loud talk greeted him. He looked around, feeling like a chameleon, forced to blend with the world of the stylish elite, with people for whom Christmas was a cause for celebration.

Anita's salon was large, airy, and modern, done in shades of gray, black, and white, much like her condo. The reception desk was glass-block with an art-deco look. The place was elegant and classy, like Anita.

Beyond the reception desk was a large room, the floor tiled with a black and white art deco pattern with stations set around the perimeter. Stylish men and women stood in small groups talking, laughing, and drinking from champagne flutes. In one corner a trio played soft Christmas music. All this glitz, glamour, and holiday excess made him want to dash out the door, but he'd promised Anita.

A waiter with a tray of champagne flutes approached. With a nod, Luke took one of the glasses. To his right appeared a thirty-something guy, blond hair to his shoulders, wearing black.

"Hello, I'm Justin, one of Anita's stylists." He scanned Luke and gave him a flirtatious smile. "And you are?"

"Luke Corrado, friend of Anita's."

"And he's all mine tonight," said a purring female voice. Elaine Cutford, wearing black slacks and a low-cut gold silk blouse, wound her arm through Luke's and gave him a smile that reminded him of a feline snagging a helpless mouse.

Grinning, Justin held up a hand. "No problem." He walked

away.

Luke extricated himself from Elaine. "I'm not really yours, Elaine. You do know that?"

"Of course, darling, but I wouldn't mind if you were."

Damn woman was a man-eater. How could Anita be friends with her?

Elaine reached up and touched the bruise on his jaw. "How did that happen, love? Even with scars, you're magnificent." Giving him another predatory smile, she stepped back and studied him. "That bruise makes you look even sexier."

"I had a little trouble with a mugger," Luke said. "That's hardly sexy."

For a split second, a calculating gleam came into Elaine's eyes. Then it was gone and she was the predator again, almost licking her lips as she watched him.

Luke shifted his stance and searched the room for Anita. When he spotted her talking with a group on the far side, he said, "Excuse me, Elaine," and strode away.

Anita looked up as he approached. Her bright smile lit her eyes and his heart. For her he'd endure this painful party. He'd been through worse, lots worse, especially in Mexico.

When he reached her, she lifted her face for his kiss. He kissed her lightly on the lips. He wanted to carry her off and make love to her all night and all day tomorrow, to keep her close and shield her from danger.

"I'm glad you made it," she said when they pulled apart. The others she'd been talking with gave them knowing smiles and walked away.

"Nice place you've got here." He set his empty glass on a nearby table.

"Thanks. I recently had it renovated. It used to be all blues and greens, but I wanted something more edgy."

"I like the art deco touches," he said.

Her eyes widened and she laughed. "I wouldn't take you for the kind of guy who knows décor."

He leaned closer and whispered in her ear. "I know lots of

things that might surprise you."

She blushed prettily. "I'll bet you do." She took his hand and led him to a table laden with delicious-smelling food. "Have something to eat."

The rest of the evening passed in a blur. Uneasy with all the trendy people, he tried to mingle, but he'd never been good at small talk. Several times he'd noticed Mace and Elaine Cutford studying him. He needed to check them out more thoroughly. They could be merely a couple into kinky sex who decided they'd like to have sex with him and Anita. The thought made him shiver with revulsion.

Finally, the party ended and Luke could relax. He'd told Anita he'd drive her home after the party, so she'd taken a taxi to the salon that morning. Now, they walked arm-in-arm to the garage where he'd parked.

"Thanks for coming, Luke. I don't always enjoy my own parties but they're a necessary part of doing business."

He put his hand over hers and pulled her closer. "Thanks for inviting me. It was certainly different from the parties I usually attend."

She looked up at him. "What kind of parties would that be?"

"None you'd feel comfortable with."

"Sounds intriguing."

They walked the rest of the way in silence. When they reached his car, his secure phone rang. He opened the car with his remote and gestured for Anita to get in.

"Sorry," he said, slipping the phone from his pocket. "I shouldn't be too long. It's business."

She got into the car and he moved to where he was sure she couldn't hear. With a feeling of dread, he answered. "Yeah, Murray."

"Took you long enough."

"I'm a little busy. What's up?"

"We got the boy."

Luke sagged against the car's trunk as the air left his lungs.

Relief and anxiety swirled through him, roiling his stomach.

"Both of them?" he asked.

"Yeah, the woman too."

"Thank God."

He'd been through hell and back more than once, yet nothing had made his hands shake like they were now at the news his son was safe.

"Where is he?" Luke managed.

"Still in Mexico, but protected. We'll bring him here, but you understand you can't be with him, not until your mission is complete."

Luke wanted to scream, "No!" but Murray was right.

"We'll let you know when he's in the area." Murray hung up.

"What is it?" Anita had gotten out of the car. "Is there a problem?"

He fought to pull himself together. "No, nothing's wrong. Just some news I was waiting for. Let's get home."

Home. But it wasn't home. Nothing was. He had a son, and no home to bring him to. His whole life was about to change.

◇◇◇

Luke was quiet, too quiet, on the drive back. Anita settled into the soft leather seat and stared out at the city flashing by. She knew Luke, yet she didn't. She was good at reading people, wouldn't have been so successful if she weren't. As with Luke, she'd felt a dark streak in John Sweeney, but much as she'd liked John, she'd had no desire to delve into his psyche. She wondered if Luke would ever let her in.

She clenched her hands on her lap. She'd enjoy Luke's company and his lovemaking. When the time came, she'd walk away. Anita ignored the jolt of regret that punched her in the stomach.

When they got to their lofts, she turned to Luke. "Come in with me? I don't want to be alone."

He brushed a gentle finger over her bottom lip. "I want to be with you tonight too."

They hurried up the steps to her door. She hastily opened it, disengaged the alarm, and engaged it again when they were

115

inside.

"I hate that alarm," she said. "It's a reminder my life isn't my own now."

"Hopefully, the police will soon find who's threatening you and you can relax."

When they'd shed their jackets, she turned to him and asked, "Do you want a drink? Coffee?"

He pulled her close and nuzzled her neck. "All I want is you."

Anita saw desire and longing in his coal-black eyes, but something else, something that made her heart pound with yearning and a little bit of fear.

"Anita," he whispered.

She put her finger over his lips. "Don't say anything. Let's just enjoy each other."

Without another word, Luke took her hand and they walked up the stairs.

When they got to her bedroom, she turned down the comforter and kicked off her high heels.

Luke pulled her around to face him. Cupping her face, he gazed deeply into her eyes. "You've become my addiction. I think about you all the time, I want you all the time."

She placed her hands over his. "I think about you all the time too. Call it an addiction or whatever you want, but I can't get enough of you." Her voice thickened. "Let me love you tonight."

With a wicked smile, he stepped back. "Have your way with me."

She splayed her hands on his chest. "I intend to. Lie on the bed."

He did as she ordered. Anita stood beside the bed and gazed down at him, at the perfection of his features, and the beauty of his smooth bronzed skin. His fathomless eyes held her. But in the depths of his eyes, she saw a deep-rooted sadness that mirrored the sadness inside her. She smiled at the irony. She and Luke, two lost souls who'd somehow found each other, but whatever they had wouldn't last. She'd learned that lesson well.

"You going to stare at me all night?" His voice, smooth and rich, flowed over her like well-aged whiskey.

"I could stare at you all night and all day. You're beautiful, Luke."

"Baby, there's a lot more to me than looks. Care to find out?"

"I look forward to finding out all I can about Luke Corrado." She sat on the bed next to him and began to slowly unbutton his white shirt.

She kissed each inch of his firm skin as she exposed it, nipping and licking, tasting salt and drinking in his warm, spicy scent. When she had the shirt unbuttoned, she slipped it from the waistband of his jeans and unbuttoned the cuffs. He helped her pull it off him.

She spread his legs and knelt between them. His erection was outlined through the tight jeans. He shifted, his movements making his well-toned chest muscles ripple. She smoothed a hand down his chest with its sprinkling of dark hairs, reveling in his masculinity and strength. Anita had always loved the male body, and Luke's was the most exquisite she'd ever seen.

With his help, her hands trembling slightly, she made quick work removing the rest of his clothes. Settling back, she gazed at his glorious nakedness. He closed his eyes, and she suspected he fought to control himself. When she reached out to stroke his thick, hard erection, he opened his eyes, his breathing shallow.

She gripped his penis with her hand and stroked up and down. A tiny pearl of moisture beaded on the tip. When she bent to take him into her mouth, he arched up to meet her. She took in as much of him as she could, sucking and licking while her hand stroked him.

Intoxicated by Luke's taste and feel, and by her need for him that threatened her well-ordered existence, her very soul, Anita sucked and pulled on him, harder and faster. She wanted only to please him, to take away whatever pain lurked in his heart, if even for a little while. His moans told her he was on the edge. He pushed her away.

"Stop," he ground out.

"I want you to come."

"I will, baby, but you first. Get your clothes off."

Anita tore off her clothes and flung them onto the floor. She reached into her night table drawer and pulled out a packet.

"Prepared, I see," he said, a sinful glint in his eyes.

"Always." After she rolled protection on him, she positioned herself over him. He gripped her hips and lifted her onto his hard erection. She was so wet, he slid in easily. Leaning over with her palms against the mattress, she pushed until he was deep inside her. She sat up and moved slowly up and down, savoring his potency and beauty, surrendering her soul to him.

"Baby, stop teasing," he growled.

Rocking her hips, she thrust deeply, hard and fast. Every thrust increased her need for him and freed a little more of her heart.

Groaning her name, he reached out to massage her breasts. Her world spiraled out of control. Nothing existed except her and Luke and the desire that rushed in a fevered pace through her.

Her climax built, a raging crescendo of molten heat, overtaking all her senses. Crying out his name, she exploded over and over. He cried out with his own climax.

Finally, she collapsed on top of him. Only the sheen of their sweat-soaked bodies separated them. He wound both arms around her and hugged her tight.

She rained kisses on his jaw and the smooth column of his throat, loving him, needing him in a way that thrilled and scared her. With Luke, she felt whole, as if her body and soul recognized him, had been waiting for him. Not wanting to dive too deeply into that line of thought, she gently kissed the tattoo on his bulging right bicep. With a groan, his mouth claimed hers again in a hard, hungry kiss that left her shaking.

After long minutes, they pulled apart, and she rolled off. Luke grabbed the bedclothes and covered them.

Anita lay in his embrace and faced him. She skimmed a

finger over his lips. "Can you spend the night?"

His eyes softened. "Are you sure you want me to stay? You looked uncomfortable the last time."

She searched his eyes and knew she couldn't let him go, not yet, not for a long time. "I want to wake up with you."

CHAPTER EIGHTEEN

Four days later, Luke felt like a kid going on his first date. He'd faced hardened criminals with less trepidation than meeting a two-and-a-half-year old. Too wound up to sit and feeling like a caged tiger, he stalked back and forth in the small room at FBI headquarters in Philly and waited for the social services person to bring his son.

When they'd rescued the little boy and Adelina, she'd elected to stay in Mexico, and two of their agents escorted her back to her family's home in the south while other agents smuggled Miguel out of the country. Luke hoped Adelina would be safe. He owed her.

He'd spoken to her on the phone and she'd told him how Maria had given her the phone and begged her to protect her son and to call Luke if Miguel was in danger.

Like a hammer to his skull, guilt pounded Luke anew. He should have been there for Maria, should have found a way to take her with him that first time when he'd been forced to flee. He sank onto the one chair in the room, an old-fashioned wooden one. The chair dug into his back and he welcomed the discomfort as a small punishment for his wrongs.

He pulled the dog-eared piece of paper from his pocket and unfolded it. Adelina had given the letter, addressed to Luis Correa, to the men who'd rescued her and Miguel. Luke scrubbed a hand over his face, and, for the hundredth time, read Maria's flowing script, written in Spanish.

Luis, Mi Amor,
My love, if you are reading this, it means I am probably dead.

I gave this letter to Adelina and asked her to deliver it to you if any-thing happens to me. I am so sorry for everything. I never wanted my brother to find out about us, but somehow he did. When you disappeared, I heard things. That you were dead or that you are a Federale and went back to the United States. I know you are still alive because I feel your love surrounding me.

After you were gone, I learned I was carrying your child. I tried to hide it, but my brother found out. When our son was born, I told my brother the child died in birth, but I live in fear he will find the truth and kill me and little Miguel. Adelina took our child to live with her relatives in the mountains. Miguel will be safe there until you can come for him.

I left you messages begging you to come get me, but you have not returned my calls. I hope you are safe in the United States, and I hope you still love me. No man will ever have my heart as you do, my Luis.

I am in hiding from my brother in the cabin where you and I made sweet love and where we pledged to be together always. I gave my phone to Adelina in case you call. If my brother finds it and learns I've tried to reach you, he will kill me for sure. I hope and pray you will call and that you will come for me and our son.

Forever yours, my Luis.
Your Maria

His throat thick, Luke folded the letter and put it back into his jacket pocket. Maria had died not knowing his real name. He hadn't wanted to leave Mexico without her, but his wounds in-flicted by Mendoza's men were too great and he'd had a job to do. He was sure he'd convinced Mendoza's men he hadn't touched Maria, that she'd be safe until he could return for her. If he'd known about her pregnancy...

When he'd finally gone to Mexico to rescue her, Mendoza had been waiting.

Luke had no more time to think as the door to the small room opened. His palms sweaty, he jumped up from the chair and prepared to face his son. A middle-aged woman entered, holding a small boy by the hand. Speechless, Luke could only stare.

The boy had Luke's dark brown, almost black, eyes, and his thick black hair. His skin was olive, like Luke's. Maria had been fairer-skinned, and her eyes light brown. Miguel looked like pictures of himself at that age.

Eyes wide with fright, the child clung to the woman's hand. Luke's heart stuttered. Forcing a smile, he walked slowly toward them. Miguel buried his head against the woman's pants-clad thigh.

"It's okay, Miguel," the woman said in Spanish. "Mr. Luke won't hurt you. Tell him hello."

Miguel turned his large eyes to Luke. The boy's bottom lip trembled. Luke wanted to grab his son and hold him tight, but if he did he'd scare him to death.

Instead, he knelt in front of the boy and smiled. "Hello, Miguel," he said in Spanish. "My name is Luke and I'm very glad to meet you." Luke put out his hand to touch his son, but Miguel winced, and Luke quickly withdrew.

The little boy wrapped his arms around the woman's thigh and stared at Luke.

Luke swallowed around the lump in his throat and stood. Facing the woman, he said in English, "Does he know who I am?"

"Not yet," she answered. "We wanted him to meet you first. Social Services has placed him with a Spanish-speaking family. They have your picture and will show it to him every day and explain you're his father. We want him to get used to the idea a little at a time. The family will also teach him English. We understand that due to your work you're not able to take him yet. When your bosses say it's okay, we'll arrange short, supervised meetings between you and Miguel to help him get to know you." She patted the boy's head and her eyes softened. "He's been through a lot. He asks for Adelina all the time. "

Luke glanced away, fighting tears. The last time he'd cried was the day his father walked out. He'd been a few years older than Miguel at the time.

"I need to take him back now," the woman said. "We don't want to tire him or upset him too much."

Turning to her, Luke nodded. He bent again to face his son. "You and I are going to be friends, Miguel," he said in Spanish. "We'll have fun together." He placed his hand gently on Miguel's head. Instead of the smile Luke hoped for, the little boy screeched and jerked away.

"Adelina, Adelina!" Miguel screamed.

The woman picked up Miguel and cradled him. She looked at Luke with pity in her eyes. "We'd better go."

"Good-by, son," Luke whispered as they walked out. He sank onto the chair, his heart in tatters.

◇◇◇

"What the hell happened back there?" The boss spun around to face Gordon.

"It looked like a piece of cake, boss," he said. "Sweeney's shop is unsecured. Breaking in was easy. How the hell did we know that jerk would come in and ruin it, and call the cops?" He rubbed a hand down his face, wiping off the sweat. "Good thing I was outside or they woulda caught me. The guys they got know they'd better not squeal. We don't need to worry about them."

"Who the fuck was that guy who played hero?" the boss asked.

"Maybe a concerned citizen?" Gordon answered, hoping he could get the boss off his ass.

The boss snorted and paced the cavernous room at the warehouse. "No *concerned citizen* gives a damn about break-ins or anything else. Did your men get a look at the guy?"

Gordon shrugged. "They said he's powerfully built, tall, Hispanic-looking."

"Hispanic, huh?" The boss looked thoughtful. "Law enforcement?"

"Couldn't tell."

"Sounds like the description of the Santisi bitch's boyfriend, the guy who worked over your men before. But why would he be at Sweeney's?"

"Coincidence?"

"I don't believe in coincidence," the boss said. "If he interferes again, take him out."

"We'll take care of him, boss. And the woman too."

"After we get that list, we'll take care of the woman. Not before."

◇◇◇

Anita slipped off her stilettos. With a grateful sigh, she sank onto her sofa to rub her aching feet. Standing all day in high heels took a toll, but her clients expected her to look stylish. It had been a long day at the shop. She couldn't wait until tomorrow, Christmas Eve. They'd close early, and the shop would stay closed until two days after Christmas. She needed a break.

And she needed to see Luke. She hadn't seen him since the night of her staff party, five days ago. They'd made hot, sweet love, and she'd let him stay over for the second time. Luke was becoming special to her, a friend she felt close to, someone she could depend on, a man whose kisses and touches she craved. Like an obsession, she wanted more and more of him. She was falling for him. As much as that thought frightened her, the thought of Luke walking out of her life frightened her more. How the hell had she let this happen?

Luke had called a few times to say he was busy with his consulting job, trying to wrap up things before the holidays. Yet, she'd detected hesitation in his tone. Much as she told herself his secrets weren't her concern, she wanted to trust him, and wanted him to trust her with those secrets.

Thankfully, things had been quiet, no more break-ins or attempted abductions. Maybe whoever was responsible knew she had a security detail watching her.

Luke promised to come with her to her family's annual Christmas Eve bash. She hoped he didn't stand her up. If he did, she'd make some excuse to her family so they wouldn't know her hurt.

"Why are you thinking like that?" she said to the empty room. Sheesh, had she so little faith in Luke that she'd convinced herself he wouldn't keep his word?

Her cell phone rang and she dug it out of her purse. When she looked at the ID, a twinge of disappointment shot through her. Logan, not Luke. Logan was family and she loved him, but she wanted Luke.

"Hey, Logan. Are you guys here?"

"We just arrived at Dan and Lena's. Dorie's feeding the baby." Logan chuckled. "He didn't like the long flight."

"Poor baby. Give him a kiss for me. I can't wait to see you guys tomorrow. What's up?"

"You asked me to check on Luke Corrado."

Chewing her lip, she sat on the edge of the sofa cushion. "What did you find?"

"Not much. Corrado's family lived in one of the barrios outside town. Bad place. Corrado lived with his mother and sister. The father took off years ago. The sister was involved with a gangbanger and was killed in a gang shootout, and the mother is dead. Corrado left town right after high school. One rumor is he went to college."

Anita stiffened. "What's the other rumor? I know there is one."

Logan sighed. "Not many from that neighborhood go to college. Unfortunately, the other rumor is he joined a Mexican drug cartel."

Anita closed her eyes, digesting what she'd heard.

"I'd be careful around him, Anita."

"He's coming to the party tomorrow night. And to Aunt Lena's and Uncle Dan's for Christmas dinner."

"Be cautious," Logan said. "Something doesn't feel right. That other guy you were dating, Sweeney, shows up dead. And now you're with Corrado, who may or may not have gang ties. Sounds like you're running with the wrong people. We worry about you."

Anita shivered. "You know me. I'm always careful. Please don't tell Doriana what you found. She'll only worry."

"Too late. Dorie knows. We don't keep secrets from each

other. Not anymore."

Logan referred to the fact he hadn't known he had a son until Josh was sixteen. But Doriana and Logan were happy now, the past buried.

"Thanks, Logan. Tell Doriana hello and kiss the kids for me."

She hung up with Logan and padded into the kitchen for a glass of wine and something light for dinner. Like everyone else during the holidays, she'd been eating too much sugar. Clients brought in cookies and cakes for her and the staff, and she'd indulged more than she should have.

The doorbell rang. She set down the salad mix she'd taken out of the refrigerator and hurried to answer. When she looked through the peephole, Luke smiled at her. Her heart pounded at the sight of him. Logan's words floated back to her, throwing ice water on her joy.

She disengaged the alarm, opened the door to let Luke in, and reset the alarm. Just inside the door, they stood facing each other. Like a woman starved, her greedy gaze swallowed him. Snow had begun falling, and his coal black hair was sprinkled with snowflakes. A dark blue scarf wound around his neck, and he wore his usual black leather jacket. His indigo jeans hugged his long, muscular legs. Every cell in her body wanted his arms wrapped around her, wanted his heat, his comfort, his strength.

"Like what you see?" he asked with a chuckle.

"You know I do."

He laughed and held up a brown paper bag. "I got us a couple of cheesesteaks from South Philly."

She groaned and put a hand over her stomach. "I'm going to weigh a ton when the holidays are over."

He strode over to the glass-topped coffee table, set down the bag, and held out his arms. "Come here."

She snuggled into his embrace. Pleasure worked its way through her, and she sighed.

He held her tight and nuzzled her neck. His warm breath soothed her.

"You'll look perfect to me no matter how much you weigh," he whispered.

A small kernel of doubt opened in her. Could Luke be involved in something illegal, dangerous?

CHAPTER NINETEEN

Jo and Franco's townhouse in Philadelphia's historic Society Hill looked like an Edwardian Christmas picture, with candles in each window spreading a golden glow over the light covering of snow on the ground. Happiness, like a soft cashmere shawl, settled over Anita when she and Luke pulled up in front of the house. Her bliss at having him with her surpassed her nervousness about introducing him to her family. For tonight she'd put aside her fears that he might be involved in something dark and dangerous. She had to be cautious, yet the Luke she was coming to know was a good man. She couldn't be wrong about him.

Jo and Franco had hired valets to park the guests' cars in a private garage nearby. Luke slipped out of the driver's side of his sedan and the valet opened the passenger door for Anita. As Anita and Luke walked up the steps, he put his arm on the small of her back. His touch heated her through the heavy layers of her clothes.

A butler hired for the occasion answered the door and took their coats. A waiter handed them each a glass of wine. Anita inhaled the spicy, sweet scents of the food—chicken, roast beef, ham, condiments, cakes and cookies—mingled with the holiday scents of holly, cinnamon, and bayberry. Memories of past Christmases with her parents before they'd been so suddenly torn from her made melancholy settle in Anita's chest. With effort, she pushed aside her sadness. Tonight was a celebration with the family that had tried so hard to fill the void in her heart and soul.

Jo, radiant in a red silk dress that somehow worked with her auburn hair, hurried over. She threw her arms around Anita and hugged her. Pulling back, she smiled and said, "Merry Christmas, cuz."

Anita returned Jo's warm smile. "Merry Christmas to you, cuz."

Jo turned to Luke. "Nice to see you again." She gave him a quick hug.

Anita suppressed a smile at Luke's look of discomfort. She wondered if he felt awkward being hugged by a pregnant woman or if being around her family made him anxious. Her smile faded as she remembered Luke's dislike of Christmas. Maybe all this holiday cheer had the opposite effect on him. How sad. She'd have to find a way to make him appreciate the holiday again.

Franco rushed over and greeted them, giving Anita a hug and shaking hands with Luke.

"The food's in the dining room," Franco said. "Help yourselves."

As Anita and Luke strode toward the dining room, she spotted Doriana bending down to talk to Nonna. Their fragile grandmother, in a pale blue dress, her white hair brushed softly back from her face, sat in an upholstered chair, the family matriarch surveying her kingdom.

Anita took Luke's hand and led him toward her grandmother and Doriana.

Doriana straightened as they approached. Wearing a dark green satin blouse, black skirt, and strappy black sandals, she was the epitome of elegance with an edge of sexuality. Her long, thick black hair framed her oval face, large, caramel-colored eyes, and full lips.

With a big smile, she hugged Anita before turning to Luke with an expectant look.

"Luke, this is my cousin Doriana Tanner, who lives in Tucson. Doriana, this is Luke Corrado. He grew up in Tucson."

Luke stiffened for a fleeting second before he smiled and shook hands with Doriana. "Nice to meet you."

"You, too. Where in Tucson did you grow up?"

"Not a very nice place. I doubt you've heard of it."

Although Doriana knew where Luke had grown up, her cousin was trying to make small talk, and maybe get a little more information from Luke.

Luke's voice had tensed, and Anita suspected he didn't want to talk about Tucson. Trying to deflect the tension, she drew him toward Nonna. When she bent to kiss her grandmother's parchment-like cheek, sadness swirled through her. They wouldn't have their beloved Nonna around for too many more Christmases.

"Nonna, this is my friend Luke Corrado." Anita straightened. "Luke, my grandmother, Marie Santisi."

Luke smiled. "Hello, Mrs. Santisi."

"Call me Nonna." The older woman gave Luke a bright smile and turned to Anita. "He's a handsome one, isn't he?"

A slow burn started at Anita's neck and spread to her face.

Nonna laughed. Shooing them away with a wave of her hands, she said, "*Mangiare*, eat, eat." Her gaze scanned Anita. "You need some food. You're too skinny."

Luke wound his arm around Anita's waist and pulled her close. "I think Anita's perfect."

"You must keep this one, Anita," Nonna said.

Doriana laughed and caught Anita's gaze. Anita's face grew hotter.

Fifteen minutes later, Anita and Luke stood in the kitchen eating lasagna and meatballs and drinking Chianti. Other guests were in the large, open kitchen too, laughing and talking. The intimacy of the homey, warm room made it a favorite place to congregate. Logan came in and smiled when he saw Anita.

Not for the first time, Anita admired Logan's good looks. His dark blond hair was streaked with gray now and there were a few more fine lines around his hazel eyes, but he was still one of the most handsome men she'd ever seen. Doriana was one lucky woman. Logan was crazy in love with his wife, and he was a great father to their three children. Regret for her own dashed dreams rolled through Anita.

"Anita, Merry Christmas." Logan gave her a peck on the

cheek.

She introduced him to Luke. As the men shook hands, Logan studied Luke and Anita guessed he was thinking about what he'd found on Luke's background.

"I hear you're from Tucson," Logan said. "I live near Butterfly Peak. What part of the city are you from?"

Luke tensed. "Centro Barrio."

"Rough place," Logan said.

"I survived."

"You're one of the lucky few who got out," Logan said.

Luke shrugged. "A college scholarship was my ticket."

"Good for you." Logan's smile didn't reach his eyes. He was more formal with Luke than Anita had seen him with others. Did he believe Luke could be a drug dealer? Anita wouldn't, couldn't think about that now. Luke hid parts of himself, but she recognized an innate goodness in him. He couldn't be involved in anything illegal.

Much later, as Luke conversed with Uncle Dan on the other side of the living room, Anita stood next to Nonna's chair with Doriana and Aunt Lena.

"Your Luke is very nice," Nonna said. "I can see he cares for you."

"He does seem to care for you," Doriana said. "He's smokin', that's for sure." Her caramel eyes locked with Anita's. "Be careful. We don't want you hurt again."

Anita sipped her wine before answering. "I won't be hurt. And I'm always careful."

"I like Luke." Aunt Lena touched Anita's arm. "We all want you to be happy, dear. It's your turn."

"I'm happy for my cousins, but marriage, kids, all that, isn't for me." *Liar*, a small voice whispered inside her head.

"I like Luke too, but, well, you know," Doriana said.

Doriana couldn't voice her concerns about Luke in front of Aunt Lena and Nonna.

Well past midnight, Anita and Luke left the party. Too buoyed-up to sleep, she hoped Luke would spend the night with her. She needed him, wanted his companionship. She refused to question why.

When they reached her door, Luke stood with his back to the street as if shielding her. A shiver ran up her spine. Shielding her from what? She'd asked Jo and Harris to let her bodyguard go tonight so the poor man could spend Christmas Eve with his family. Luke would keep her safe.

In the dim overhead light, Luke's eyes glittered with desire. A surge of anticipation moved through her and settled in her lower parts.

"Come in, Luke. Stay with me."

"You're sure?"

She nodded.

Once they entered, she secured the house and slipped off her coat. Anita started toward the kitchen but Luke grabbed her arm, stopping her. He pulled her to him, his arms circling her waist. "Where do you think you're going?"

"The kitchen."

He shot her a wicked grin. "No, you're not." His lips captured hers in an urgent kiss that slammed the breath out of her. An ache built between her legs and she clung to him, deepening the kiss, savoring his taste of wine and coffee, and drinking in his warm, spicy scent.

He left her lips, crushed her against him, and buried his face in her hair. "Oh, God, Anita, I want you more every day."

"Luke." Her yearning for him filled her voice, hovered in the air between them.

They tore off their clothes and scattered them on the stairs as they headed to her bedroom. Clad only in their underwear, they turned to each other when they got to her room.

Luke skimmed his fingers over the tops of her breasts. Her skin tingled where he touched.

He cupped her face between his hands. "You are everything a man could want—beautiful, desirable, smart, loving." He kissed the corners of her mouth. "You're everything this man wants."

Her soul needed him. Her body craved him. Her heart imploded at his words. How could she ever walk away from him?

She held out her arms. "Make love to me."

Their lovemaking was slow, sweet, tender, exploring, as if they wanted to savor every moment they had together, wanted to learn all they could about each other's bodies. With every touch of his lips and fingers, every kiss and caress, she gave up a little more of her fear, a little more of her heart.

Spent, they lay entwined in each other's arms. Anita flung a leg over one of Luke's and snuggled closer. The last time she'd felt so content, so satisfied, so happy was the last time she and Luke had made love. She'd never felt this joy, need, and fulfillment with Kent, and she'd planned on spending her life with him.

Luke kissed her temple and adjusted the covers closer around them.

"Merry Christmas, Luke."

"Merry Christmas, sweetheart."

They'd agreed not to exchange gifts, but now she wished she had one for him, something that would make him happy, that would make him remember this Christmas, remember her.

She gave him a tender hug, letting him know how much he was coming to mean to her. She scooted to the other side of the bed and propped herself on her elbow, facing him.

"Why don't you like this holiday?" she asked.

Propping himself on his elbow, he faced her. "I have my reasons."

"I'm crazy about you, Luke. I want to know you, all of you. Tell me about the real Luke Corrado."

A shuttered look came into his eyes and he lay back down, staring at the ceiling. "There's not much to tell. My father left the family when I was five. My mom worked long hours for several of the rich families in town to support my sister and me. Christmas wasn't fun in our house. We didn't have money, and most of all, we didn't have the loving family you do."

Anita sidled closer and leaned over him. Her hair brushed his chest. "Luke, I'm so sorry."

"Don't be. I'm okay with it." He twirled strands of her hair around his finger. "I like your family. I don't know that I've ever been around such a loving family. I get the impression you'd do anything for each other. Not many people have that. You're very lucky."

"I am."

His leaned up and kissed her. "It's your turn," he said as he lay back down. "What happened to your parents?"

She flopped over to lie on her back. "My parents were killed in a car crash when I was fifteen."

"Sweetheart, I'm sorry."

Hot tears pricked her eyes. "It was a long time ago, but I still miss them, especially at the holidays. Nonna took me in. I lived with her until I was twenty-one. Aunt Lena and Uncle Dan also helped raise me. They paid for my tuition at the same private high school Doriana and Franco attended."

"Generous," Luke said.

"My family did all they could to help me and love me, but I've always felt the void my parents' deaths left. I would see my cousins with their parents and know what I was missing."

Luke gathered her into his arms and settled her over him. He brushed hair back from her face and hooked the strands behind her ears. "My poor baby. I wish I could take away your hurt."

"I've dealt with it. I don't usually tell people how I feel. My family doesn't even know how much I miss my parents. But I wanted to tell you."

"You trust me. Thank you for that."

She brushed a light kiss on his lips.

"Tell me about Logan and Doriana," he said. "What's their story? They seem young to have a kid Josh's age."

An edge had come into his voice when he mentioned the other couple, and Anita wondered if it had anything to do with Tucson and the information Logan had dug up. She pushed aside the little voice of caution in her mind and rolled off Luke to lie on her back again. "Doriana had Josh when she was seventeen and Logan nineteen. Logan didn't know he had a son until about five years ago."

Beside her Luke stiffened and released an audible breath.

"What's wrong?" she asked, turning to face his strong hawk-like profile.

"I'm surprised he didn't know."

"Logan left town before Doriana could tell him. He came back five years ago and helped Uncle Dan catch the person sabotaging his company."

"There's a story there, but for another day. I want to know something else now." Luke sat up and pulled her with him. She stared at his muscled chest, the smooth bronze skin, the smattering of dark hairs. She shivered, from the coolness in the room and from the excitement that swirled through her when she looked at him.

They leaned against the headboard, and he brought the covers up to cocoon them both.

Nestling against him, she raised her gaze to his. "What do you want to know?" At the intense look in his eyes, her heart fluttered.

"Who hurt you?"

She swallowed. "What do you mean?"

"You come from a close and loving family, yet you say you don't want marriage and kids. Yes, you're a smart, successful business owner, and you have a lot to be proud of, but there's something deeper going on with you. I sensed it from the first time I met you. Who did this to you? Who damaged you?"

Turning away, she said, "You're very perceptive."

He touched her chin until she faced him again. "I'm perceptive because I care for you. Someone hurt you."

She couldn't explain it, but she felt an overwhelming need to unburden herself to Luke. Maybe it was the understanding in his deep brown eyes or the softness of his mouth, or the tenderness when he held her, but she wanted to tell him.

She settled more comfortably in his arms and stared across the room. The framed picture over the bed reflected back at her from the large mirror that topped her dresser. Although she stared at the painting, a different picture rolled through her head.

"When I graduated from high school, I attended beauty school," she began. "Aunt Lena and Uncle Dan wanted to send me to college, but I'd always wanted to do hair and to someday have my own salon. I took business classes at night at the community college."

Still not looking at Luke, she pulled the comforter closer around her neck. "When I got a job at a top salon, I moved out of Nonna's house and into a small apartment in center city Philly. I was flying high with my new freedom and the money I was making. One night I went out with friends to one of the city's trendy spots and met Kent. He was in medical school at Jefferson. I fell head over heels almost immediately. And he said he felt the same way." She flattened a palm to her stomach at the memory of his betrayal.

Next to her, Luke tensed, but he remained silent.

"Kent soon moved in with me. Because he was in medical school, I paid all the bills for the apartment. We planned to marry as soon as he got his residency. I put aside money every month for the house we'd buy. I've always been good with money and I managed to save a nice sum."

She closed her eyes, seeing Kent's handsome, lying face, reliving the pain. "He'd go home to Oklahoma every holiday and whenever he could. He never took me there or invited his family to our place when they visited Philly. That hurt."

Releasing a bitter laugh, she said, "We lived together for a couple of years, yet I never met his family. That should have been my first clue something was wrong. He said he didn't tell them about me or that we lived together because they were very religious and would frown on our relationship. And I swallowed all of that. What a fool I was."

Luke kissed the top of her head and put his arm around her shoulders, drawing her closer.

"I got better and better jobs as I started getting a reputation as a good stylist, and I was making great money," she continued. "Kent was sure he'd get a residency at a hospital in Philly and we'd stay here. I found a perfect location for the salon I always wanted to open. I would have to use a little from the house fund for the down payment on the salon, but I felt it was worth it."

Anita shuddered. "What happened next is ugly. It's been years, but it still hurts." She clenched her fingers around the end of the comforter. "And it still makes me damn angry."

"What happened?" Luke asked quietly.

"You'd think after all this time…anyway, I went to his medical school graduation, although he'd tried to keep me from going, saying he had only two tickets, for his parents. But he promised to take us all to dinner later and I'd get to meet them."

She gave a disgusted shake of her head. "What a pack of lies. A client had an extra ticket and gave it to me. I wanted to surprise Kent so I didn't tell him. I surprised him all right. You should have seen the look on his face when I showed up. He was forced to introduce me to his parents and his fiancée. He tried to pass me off as a friend, but I don't think he fooled them."

"What?" Luke sat straighter. "He had a fiancée?"

"Yup. That's why he never took me home with him. He got me quickly away from them and led me to a deserted section of the gym where they'd held the graduation. That's when it got uglier. Said he planned to tell me about the fiancée but hadn't gotten around to it. But he really liked screwing me, and having sex with me was so much better than with his frigid fiancée, so he wanted to keep me around as his friend with benefits."

"That sonofabitch." Luke pounded the bed with his fist.

"Of course, I told him to go to hell. I never saw him again, but I heard he's practicing medicine in Oklahoma."

"What a piece of scum." Luke gathered her to him and brushed feather-soft kisses on her temple. "It's okay, baby. You're too good for him."

She pulled away to meet his gaze. "That wasn't all. I'd foolishly put our house fund in a joint bank account. He cleaned it out, all the money I'd saved with no help from him. I was broke. I lost the salon I wanted. All that work, all those savings, gone. I heard Kent and his bride went to Tahiti for their honeymoon. On my money, I'm sure. I never told my family about the money. I was too humiliated."

"That sonofabitch," Luke said again. "If I ever get my hands on him, he'll be sorry he ever met you."

Anita laughed. "Good thing he doesn't live around here anymore. I wouldn't want you to go to prison."

Luke laughed too. "I'd make it look like an accident."

She cuddled against him again. "I've recovered. I've done really well for myself. Elaine and Mace Cutford saved me. Elaine had been my client at the salon where I worked. I couldn't tell my family that Kent cleaned me out, but I confided in her. With Elaine's help, I found another salon and she and Mace lent me the money for the down payment and also money to renovate, and they put some in reserve to pay my employees until the salon turned a profit. I paid them back a long time ago. They're not people I enjoy being around, but I owe them. They've been good to me."

"That explains why they're your friends." He touched her face, turning her to meet his gaze. "Do you still love this Kent guy?"

"Hell, no. I stopped loving him when I realized what a rat bastard cheater he was. I feel sorry for his wife. He probably cheats on her too." She sighed. "His betrayal taught me a valuable lesson. I won't tolerate guys who lie, who pretend to be something they're not."

Luke flinched as if she'd hit him. Finally, he let out a breath and relaxed. "If you were mine," he whispered. "I'd never let you go."

He kissed her, a tender kiss that soon turned hungry. She clung to him. Her insides pulsed with need for this man, a need she'd never felt before. It scared her to death.

CHAPTER TWENTY

"Happy New Year!" The shouts of the crowd at the Borgata Casino in Atlantic City sounded like one big roar to Anita. She leaned against Luke, who stood next to her. Taking her into his arms, he looked deeply into her eyes.

"Happy New Year, sweetheart."

"Happy New Year, Luke."

His kiss was tender with an underlying edge of need. Whenever they kissed, she sensed the wildness in him, just below the surface, waiting for release—a hunger that matched an answering appetite in her for something forbidden.

They'd arrived at the Borgata, Atlantic City's most elegant casino and hotel, earlier in the day. The Cutfords, who'd decided to stay in Philadelphia for the holiday, lent them the penthouse suite they kept at the hotel. They'd also given Anita and Luke tickets to the Borgata's New Year's Eve party, the most expensive and sought-after event in town. In evening clothes, Luke and Anita mingled with other elaborately dressed guests.

Wearing a tux, Luke turned the heads of nearly every woman he passed. Feeling possessive, Anita had clung to his arm as they walked. Her shimmering gold gown with a thigh-high slit in the front, and her four-inch gold sandals, garnered attention from men too. None of that mattered. She'd have been happy if she and Luke had stayed home, wearing jeans, eating popcorn, and watching a Hallmark Christmas movie. Just being with him was enough to make joy bubble up in her. *You've got it bad, girl*, her inner voice whispered. She told herself she could walk away from Luke with her heart intact. She almost believed it.

Earlier that evening, after a sinfully rich dinner at the most upscale restaurant at the casino, Luke had played blackjack while Anita watched. He was good. Had won over $2,000, and drawn quite a crowd. Anita wondered if it was the dangerous air Luke projected or his dark, exotic looks, reminiscent of old-time elegance, which attracted the others.

Now, standing among the raucous crowd and sipping expensive champagne, she wanted only to be alone with him.

"Let's go back to the suite," she said.

"Yes," he whispered.

As soon as the doors to the private elevator swooshed closed, Luke grasped her upper arms and backed her against the mirrored wall. He kissed her, slipping his tongue into her mouth. Their tongues mated and danced while he dipped his hand into the low- cut bodice of her gown to cup her bare breast. When he rolled her hard nipple between his fingers, she let out a low moan. The elevator opened, and still clinging to each other, they headed to the penthouse door. With shaking hands, Anita took the key card from her purse and handed it to Luke. When the door opened, they practically fell into the room.

Undressing as they ran to the bedroom, they left a trail of clothes in their wake. When they got to the bedroom, Anita threw back the white satin covers on the king-size bed and climbed in. Luke settled onto the bed with her. They clung to each other, their kisses urgent and fierce. She wanted to feast on his magnificent body, to possess him, body and soul. Her body trembled with need for Luke, and only Luke. The heated area between her thighs burned for him.

"Luke," she moaned into his mouth.

He dipped his head to suckle the hard peak of one breast. Her breasts swelled, eager for his touch. He licked and nibbled his way down her body. Inflamed with lust, longing, and something unnamed that hovered just below the surface of her mind, she dug her fingers into his shoulders. All rational thought fled, and she knew only her intense desire to taste and feel more of him.

When his hand touched her mound, she opened wider, aching for him to fill her. He looked at her with eyes darkened with desire. "I can't wait any longer," he rasped.

In fluid motions, he pushed off her, grabbed a packet off the night table, pulled on protection, and positioned himself over her.

He thrust deeply into her, taking her so completely, she had no time to think, only to feel. Their coupling was hard and swift. Meeting his every thrust, her climax exploded like New Year's Eve fireworks over the Atlantic City boardwalk. Luke cried out her name as his climax overtook him.

Still holding her close, he reached down and pulled the comforter over them. Anita laid her face against his chest and inhaled his scent of musk and lovemaking. The truth she could no longer deny hit her like cold ocean water.

She loved Luke.

No, she couldn't, she wouldn't. It was too late. She loved him.

"That's the way to ring in every New Year," Luke said, disrupting her thoughts. He placed a gentle kiss on her temple. "It would be a happier world if every year, every day, started with making love."

"We'd all be too tired and too busy to wage wars."

"Or to harm each other."

◇◇◇

With Anita nestled against him, Luke settled into a more comfortable position. Holding her, making love with her felt so natural, as if they'd always belonged together. Sadness mingled with his happiness. Nothing could come of his relationship with her. He wasn't who she thought he was. When she found out the truth, would she hate him? Maybe that would make it easier to give her up. And he would have to give her up.

He wasn't the man Anita needed, a good, stable guy who'd always be there for her. He'd led a hard life. He didn't know if he could ever forget the pain of his past, forget the darkness he'd seen, forget all he'd been forced to do.

141

His son was about to change his life irrevocably. He needed to make a home for the boy. How much suffering had little Miguel seen in his young life despite the fact Adelina had assured Luke she'd done everything she could to protect him?

If that cold-blooded monster Mendoza got his hands on Miguel, the innocent child would be dead. Mendoza hadn't hesitated to murder his own sister. A child would mean nothing to him.

How the hell was Luke to provide for his son, or even think of a life with Anita, when he had no permanent home himself? The life he led was fraught with danger. How could he subject a child, a family to that? Yet, other agents had families. A sliver of hope opened in Luke.

"Why so quiet?" Anita pulled free and sat up, staring down at him. Her thick curtain of hair fell around her face. Her lips were swollen from his kisses, and her lushly-lashed eyes were wide and soft. She was beautiful and magnificent and he was falling in love. He skimmed his fingertips along her jaw line.

"I'm thinking what a beautiful, amazing, smart, sexy woman you are. And how I want to make love to you again."

She blushed, and looked younger, innocent, and sweet. He lost more of his heart.

"You're going to spoil me, Luke," she said in a husky voice.

"Always." He kissed her with all the yearning and need he was afraid to voice.

<><><>

Later that day, wearing jeans, heavy sweaters and jackets, they strolled the boardwalk. The Atlantic Ocean was gray and dull. The foaming surf, churned up by the winds, reminded Luke of a monster, eating up the sand, retreating, returning to eat again. He'd seen his share of monsters, human predators who fed on the innocent.

He pulled Anita close, wanting her heat and her goodness to destroy the monsters that lived in him. They would leave tomorrow to go back to the city. During these two days with her he could forget for a time he had a son he didn't know, that the leaders of the human trafficking cartel were out there, and that Anita was still in danger.

He would look after her and protect her with his life. He'd promised Jo and Franco he'd keep close watch over Anita, and they'd called off her security detail so the men who guarded her could spend the holidays with their families. Luke had also assured Murray he wouldn't let Anita out of his sight.

"Let's go in here," she said, taking his hand and dragging him into a large mall.

"You want to shop?" he asked.

She laughed. "No, silly, they have a great coffee shop and bakery here. I hope they're open because I'm hungry for some homemade scones."

He pulled her against him and whispered in her ear, "I'm hungry for you."

She gazed up at him. Her golden brown eyes lit with happiness. "I'm always starving for you."

How could he leave her when this job was over?

After they'd finished their cinnamon lattes and buttery scones, they walked through the mall. Most of the stores were closed for the holiday, but when Luke saw a jewelry shop that was open, he pulled her into it. If he must leave her, he wanted her to have something to remember him.

"What are you doing?" she asked.

"I want to buy you something."

She pulled back. "No. I don't want you to buy me anything. We agreed, no gifts. Besides, I can afford to buy myself whatever I want."

He brushed a kiss over her seductive pink lips. "It's no fun to buy your own jewelry."

"I've been doing it for years, and, trust me, it's fun."

A smiling salesman stood behind the counter, his expression hopeful.

"I want something that will bring out my lady's beautiful eyes," Luke said to the salesman.

When she started to protest again, Luke stopped her words

with a gentle kiss. "Let me do this."

The salesman nodded and tilted his head in thought. "Citrine and smoky topaz," he declared. "It was made for her."

Luke didn't hesitate. Moments later, he fastened the gold chain holding a large citrine and smoky topaz gem around her neck. "It matches your eyes." He pressed his lips to her collarbone.

She touched his hand and studied the gem in the mirror the salesman held. "Thank you, Luke. I love it. I need to buy a special jewel box just for it. The hand-carved box John Sweeney gave me would have been perfect, but I gave it to Jo and Franco for the baby."

Luke froze. "He gave you a jewel box?"

She frowned. "Yes. From Italy." Anita took a step back. "Oh. My. God. You don't think…?"

"We may be jumping to conclusions."

"I'll call Jo and Franco."

He grabbed her hand to stop her from pulling her phone from her purse. "No, we don't want to alarm them for nothing." He had to call Murray to send some of their men to the Callahan house to retrieve the box. That box had to contain the list. But Luke couldn't blow his cover to Anita, not yet.

She furrowed her brow. "I'll call Harris then."

"Let me call him. I have his number. Let's get back to the hotel."

Luke paid for the necklace and they left the store. He put his hand on the small of Anita's back to keep her moving. When they got to a bench inside the mall, he stopped and turned to her. "Stay here. I have to make that phone call."

"What's going on? I don't understand why you insist on calling Harris. I can do it."

"Let me handle it. Please sit for a few minutes while I make my call."

Walking to where he could be sure she was out of earshot but still watch her, he pulled out his secure phone and punched in the code for Murray who picked it up on the first ring. "What's up?"

"I think I know where the list is."

"Holy shit! Where?"

"Sweeney gave Anita a jewel box. She gave it to her cousin and his wife." He rattled off Jo and Franco's address.

"We'll get some men out there right away," Murray said.

"We need to take Jo and Franco Callahan into protective custody," Luke said.

"We're on it. Where are you?"

"Still in A.C. Heading back to the hotel now."

"Stay there. I'll call you as soon as we have the Callahans secure. We've got a safe house in the area. You can go there." Murray disconnected the call.

Anita stood as Luke approached the bench where she sat.

"Let's get to the hotel." He took her hand.

"What did Harris say?" she asked, almost running to keep up with his fast strides.

"Later." He hooked her arm through his and hurried to the boardwalk and their hotel.

As they strode, they passed a group of men coming out of one of the restaurants. Luke made eye contact with one.

The guy blinked and froze. His features hardened. "Correa," he spit out.

A weight filled Luke's chest. His muscles tensed as his body went into flight mode. The doors to the Borgata were feet away. He grabbed Anita's hand and jogged toward the hotel.

"What's going on? Why did that man call you Correa?" she asked.

"Never mind that now."

They reached the casino and hurried inside, pushing past others crowding the doors. Luke looked behind him. The men were caught in the crush of people. If Luke could lose himself and Anita in the maze of the casino, they'd stand a chance of getting to the penthouse. They'd be safe there for now.

They hurriedly threaded their way around the gaming tables and slot machines. He couldn't see the goons following them. Almost running now, they got to the penthouse elevator. The doors opened immediately and they slipped in. He rushed them into the suite and made sure the door was secured behind them.

Anita threw her purse on the sofa and faced him, her arms crossed over her chest. She was breathing heavily from their exertions. "Luke, what's going on?"

"Pour some wine for yourself. You'll need it."

"That's no answer."

"I'll tell you everything. Just give me time."

◇◇◇

Forget wine, Anita wanted answers. Luke had gone to the bedroom, leaving her in the living room. She followed him and was about to open the door when she heard him talking.

"We've got another problem," Luke was telling someone on the phone. "Couple of Mendoza's men are here. They recognized me."

Silence. Finally, Luke said, "Will do."

No more talking. Luke must have hung up. Anita opened the door. Luke was bent down, digging through the closet, his back to her. He pulled out one of his large black duffel bags. He opened the bag and drew out a handgun, then a larger gun.

She gasped. He turned.

Holding the guns, he stood.

"You brought guns?" Her heart pounded. She was seeing a whole new side of Luke, and it frightened her.

"It's my go-bag," he said. "I take it everywhere."

"Guns? Go-bag? What the hell are you talking about? Why did that man call you Correa? And who's Mendoza?" Her voice trembled.

He set the guns on the bed and walked toward her. When he reached for her, she backed away. Hurt flashed across his features before his eyes hardened.

"There's no time to explain," he said. "Some very dangerous people are after us."

Anita remembered what Logan had learned about Luke,

what the people back in Tucson whispered about him. "You're a drug dealer."

"A drug dealer?" He rubbed his hand over his hair. "Hell, no."

Anger erupted in her, propelling her to close the distance between them. "Those men outside called you Correa. That's your real name, isn't it? Oh. My. God. You lied to me about everything. I'll bet you're married too." She pounded on his solid chest with her fists. "You jerk. You bastard. How dare you lie to me, how dare you take advantage of me?"

Luke grabbed her hands, stopping her before she could pound him again. "Anita, I'm not married. My name *is* Luke Corrado, and I'm not a drug dealer." He shot her a wry smile and released her. "It's worse than that. I'm an FBI agent working a case you're involved in."

Hand over her mouth, she stepped back until she touched the wall. "Case? I'm a case? Why would I be involved with the FBI? Are they going after people for unpaid parking tickets now? I have a few of those."

Her attempt at sarcasm fell flat, only increasing the thick fog of tension in the room.

"Anita, please listen to me. We don't have a lot of time. John Sweeney was a special agent working undercover on a human trafficking case. He was tortured and murdered, but before the offenders caught him, we have reason to believe he gave you a list that's crucial to our case."

Fear brewed a nauseous mix in her stomach. She swallowed bile. She was going to be sick. "A list! That's what those people who are after me want. That's why you wanted to know what Sweeney gave me. Oh. My. God."

"We've got more immediate problems now. The guys outside knew me in Mexico as Luis Correa." He moved closer and gripped her by the shoulders. "The Agency is sending some agents over to move us to a safe place."

The sound of a door crashing open reverberated through the suite.

"Shit," Luke said. "It can't be my guys. Hide." He pushed her toward the closet. He ran to the bed and grabbed his pistol.

The bedroom door flew open. The men from the board-walk rushed in. Luke fired.

CHAPTER TWENTY-ONE

Luke's bullet hit the first guy in the chest. Blood spread on the front of the man's shirt and he crumpled to the floor. Luke fired again, hitting another intruder in the leg. Three men jumped on Luke, knocking him to the ground. His gun went flying across the room.

Anita screamed. Fueled by adrenaline, she ran toward the door. One of the men tackled her. Her head hit the floor, and everything went black.

◇◇◇

Groaning, Anita opened her eyes slowly. Her eyelids felt like they weighed ten pounds, and her head hurt like hell, as if someone jabbed her with scissors. She felt movement and realized she was in a car traveling fast. Opening her eyes fully, she gasped. On the seat next to her, Luke was slumped over, passed out. Or dead. Her heart lurched. Sweat beaded on her upper lip.

They were in the back of a limo. Two men sat in the front with darkened glass between them and the backseat.

Fear, stronger than anything she'd ever felt, filled her chest. She gulped air. She wanted to shake Luke, to rouse him, to make sure he was alive, but her hands were tied behind her back with zip ties. Shit! This wasn't looking good. She breathed in and out slowly. *Fight the fear, Anita. Fight it.*

"Luke," she whispered. "Luke, wake up." She sidled closer and nudged him with her hip. When he stirred, relief washed over her. He was alive. She nudged him again.

Moaning softly, his eyes popped open. He blinked, and sat up, wincing.

149

"Are you okay?" he whispered back, his voice raspy.

"I have a headache from hitting the floor. But I'm okay."

"I'm so sorry, sweetheart. I'll get us out of this. I won't let those sonsofbitches hurt you."

The anger that flashed in his eyes sent a chill through her. She wouldn't want to be on the receiving end of Luke's anger.

The tinted windows prevented her from seeing where they were. She nodded toward the front of the car. "Are these guys part of the human trafficking ring you and Sweeney were investigating?"

When Luke nodded, numbing fear pulsed through her again, but she fought it. She had to be strong, for both their sakes.

A muscle worked in Luke's jaw. "Trust me, and follow my lead." Pain flashed in his eyes, pain she suspected wasn't entirely physical.

She could only nod.

"We'll get out of this," he said. "If they had the list, they would have killed us back at the hotel. We need to hold on until help arrives."

"Will help arrive?"

"We'll be okay. I promise."

For comfort, she squeezed against Luke, shoulder-to-shoulder, thigh-to-thigh. Her earlier anger at his lies and deception took a back seat to the more urgent problem of staying alive.

"Luke," she whispered as another thought dawned. "The jewel box. Jo and Franco."

He shook his head, cautioning her not to say more. "They have protection. They're fine."

She leaned against the back of the seat, closed her eyes, and prayed. But she feared no amount of praying would help. Who would rescue them or even knew where they were?

After what felt like a harrowing hour with her mind conjuring up all manner of danger and death, the car slowed and came to a stop. Her fear morphed to full-blown terror. She gasped for air, struggling to stay calm.

The men in the front got out of the car, and one of them

opened the back door. "Get out," he said with a thick Spanish accent. He pointed his gun at them.

Anita recognized him as one of the men who'd attacked them at the hotel.

Luke stumbled out. Anita followed.

"Let her go, Ramon," Luke said to the guy holding the gun.

Ramon nodded smugly and smiled. "So. We meet again. We almost didn't recognize you without the long hair and beard."

"I'm who you want." Luke nodded toward Anita. "She has nothing to do with our business."

The thug laughed, an evil sound that carried in the cold air. Anita looked around. They were in some sort of industrial park—gray, damp, ugly. A nearby bridge was barely visible in the mist. The Ben Franklin. Philadelphia.

"The boss wants both of you," Ramon said. "The woman has the list. She'll cave under our *questioning*. And Mendoza has something special planned for you, Correa, or is it Corrado?" He hit Luke on the temple with the butt of his gun. Luke staggered.

"Leave him alone!" Anita screamed.

"Shut up, bitch!" Ramon slapped her across the face.

Anita tasted blood.

The second thug waved his gun and grabbed her by the arm. "Come along, *mujer*. If you're a good girl and give us what we want, we'll let you live."

Anita pulled back. The man jerked her harder. She winced at the pain in her shoulder.

"Let her go, Juan," Luke said to the guy holding her. "She doesn't have anything you want."

"She cooperates or she's dead. Like Maria," Juan said.

"You piece of scum. Maria was innocent."

"Yeah, and she had to die because of you." Ramon spit on the ground. "You soiled her. Mendoza had big plans for his sister, but after you were done with her, he couldn't sell her." Ramon gripped Luke's arm and dragged him toward a large warehouse that loomed out of the dusk. "You try anything, Corrado, and your woman is dead."

Juan pulled Anita along. She glanced up at the warehouse and shivered. Would she die in that place tonight?

They took Luke and Anita through a door in the side of the building. The door led to a large room with a cement floor. Small windows, too high to escape from, ringed the perimeter. In the middle of the room were several hard-backed chairs. Suspended from the ceiling were chains, reminding Anita of meat hooks at slaughter houses. She and Luke were being led to the slaughter. Willing steel into her spine, she straightened. She'd go down fighting.

When Juan pushed her toward one of the chairs, she stumbled and fell. He yanked her up with rough hands and threw her into the chair, grabbed a set of zip ties from the floor and tied her ankles together.

Ramon did the same to Luke.

"Let her go," Luke said again.

Ramon sneered. "Let her go so she can run to the cops? You think we're stupid?"

"We have no phones," Anita said. "Let us both go. It'll be awhile before we get to a phone. You can be long gone by then. Save yourselves. You know the police will find you."

Juan laughed. "The police will never find us, and neither will the Feds, will they, Corrado?"

"She's not involved in any of this," Luke said.

Ramon laughed. "Not involved? She was Sweeney's bitch, and now she's yours. Sweeney gave her the list." He turned to Anita. "Tell us what you did with it, and you're free to go." Sneering, he looked at Luke. "But Corrado here—Mendoza has a score to settle with him."

"How did you know where to find us?" Luke asked.

"The boss has ways," Ramon said. "And you don't want to make the boss angry."

A door Anita hadn't noticed before opened and a short, bullish man strode toward them. He walked to Luke and spat in his face.

The guy wiped his mouth on his sleeve and took a step

back, cracking his knuckles, the sound menacing in the cavernous room. His face twisted with rage, making the scar that ran from his left eye to his chin appear to move. Glaring at Luke, he said, "We meet again, Correa, or Corrado. I don't give a fuck what your name is. You seduced my sister and got her pregnant with your gringo brat. I would have gotten a high price for a virgin like her, until you defiled her." He punched Luke in the jaw. Luke's head snapped back.

Anita screamed and struggled to free herself. The bullish guy turned to her. "So you're his new whore. Before you die, I'll have my turn with you, while your boyfriend watches. Payback for what he did to my Maria."

"Maria and I were in love, Mendoza," Luke said. "We planned to get married."

Mendoza grabbed Luke's face between his hands, squeezing until Luke began to turn red, before releasing him. "I would never allow my sister to marry a gringo, and a *Federale* at that. She paid and now you're gonna pay. And your woman with you. And if we find your brat, he's dead."

Anita's jumbled mind couldn't take in everything. Who was Maria? Luke had a child? He'd lied to her about so much, but none of that mattered now. They'd never make it out of here alive.

"You're scum, Mendoza," Luke spat out. "You've got the blood of countless innocent women and children on your hands. You can kill me today but that won't stop my government from going after you. And they'll find you."

Mendoza punched Luke hard in the face. A trickle of blood oozed from his nose.

"Hang him," Mendoza ordered the other men.

Luke tried to fight them off, but it was useless. They pulled him up and pushed the chair away. It clattered on the cement, the sound echoing through the room, a harbinger of menace that sent chills through Anita.

They tied Luke's hands to one of the chains hanging overhead and used a pulley to hoist the chain higher, securing it with hooks mounted in the wall. Luke swung in the air, a few feet off the ground.

"Stop," Anita said. "Don't hurt him any more."

Mendoza strode to her and bent down until their faces were inches apart. She choked at the strong odor of whiskey on his breath.

He grabbed her chin and squeezed. Pain shot through her. "Unless you tell us where the list is, we have a special torture just for you."

Rage surged through Anita, tightening her muscles, her blood pounding in her ears. She spit in his face.

A shocked expression in his eyes, Mendoza released her and straightened, but gave her a menacing smile. "You're a spirited one. I'll enjoy breaking you."

"Mendoza, this is between us." Pain colored Luke's voice. "She doesn't know anything about the list."

Mendoza walked to where Luke hung. "She's with you, she was with Sweeney. She's in it up to her pretty ass."

"Let us go," Anita pleaded. "You can get away before the FBI finds you. You'd be free to continue leading the human trafficking gang."

He laughed. "What makes you think I'm the leader?"

"Aren't you?"

"No, I am," said a female voice.

CHAPTER TWENTY-TWO

Elaine Cutford strode through the side door.

Unable to comprehend what Elaine had just said, Anita cried out, "Elaine! Help us, please."

Elaine's high heels clicked on the cement floor as she approached Anita and Luke. Conservatively dressed in a tailored shirt and slacks, Elaine's blue eyes held a steely glint as she looked down at Anita. Elaine raised her hand and slapped Anita across the face.

"I've wanted to do that to you for a long time for the way my husband's always looking at you." With a satisfied smirk, Elaine stepped back.

Blood trickled down Anita's chin. "You have blue eyes," she blurted. "Not green."

"For a smart woman, you're incredibly stupid," Elaine said. "Ever hear of contacts? Think I'd show my true colors to you?" She threw back her head and laughed, the movement making her long red-blonde hair trail down her back.

When Elaine stopped laughing, she looked up at Luke. "Even beat up, you're smokin'. Too bad you didn't take my offer. I could have shown you things in bed that would make your bitch here look like a virgin. What a shame I have to kill such a sexy guy."

"Kill?" Anita's brain was having a hard time wrapping around Elaine as the leader of an international human trafficking gang. "What's going on, Elaine? Is this some sort of sick joke?"

Elaine's chuckle made the fine hairs on Anita's arms stand on end.

"You don't get it, do you?" Elaine asked. "Did you really think I was the insipid woman interested only in fashion?" She looked over at Luke again. "And hard-muscled young guys?"

Elaine waved a hand over her body. "How could anyone who looked like me, with this body, and my sexy clothes, be the leader of an international crime syndicate? A clever disguise, don't you think? Too bad you got involved with the wrong men. I'll miss your hairstyling skills." She patted her hair. "I'll have to find another hairdresser, but I think Justin will do just as well."

Licking her collagen-enhanced ruby lips, Elaine glanced over at Luke, then back to Anita. "I can't say I blame you for wanting to jump this one's bones. He's yummy." She released an exaggerated sigh. "Oh, well, the cost of doing business. Even the pretty ones have to go sometime."

Elaine reached down and fingered the citrine and topaz pendant hanging from Anita's neck. Anita flinched.

"Pretty," Elaine said, running a hand over the stone. "Did lover boy give it to you? It's too pretty to bury with you. Maybe I'll keep it."

"I'd like a turn with Anita before we kill her." A sneering Mace Cutford strolled through the side door, followed by a tall, barrel-chested guy carrying a gun. Mace barely glanced at Luke, but headed straight for Anita.

Bending down, he grabbed her face between his hands and kissed her, forcing her lips open and thrusting his tongue into her mouth. Anita struggled against him, but he kept kissing her. She bit his tongue.

He yelped and jumped back.

Anita spit, trying to get the taste of him out of her mouth.

"You're gonna pay for that," he growled.

"You won't get away," Luke said to Elaine. "We'll hunt you down, you evil piece of shit."

"Is that any way to talk to a lady? I thought you had more manners than that."

"Now I know how Mendoza's men found us," Luke said. "Did you plan this all along?"

Frowning at Luke's calm tones, Anita guessed he was playing for time.

Elaine's features hardened. Gone was the perfectly coiffed society matron. In her place stood the criminal toughened by life and by her own avarice. Anita shivered.

"I always suspected you weren't what you seemed," Elaine said to Luke. "I admit you fooled even me for a time. At first I figured you for a smooth-talking scam artist. But I knew something more was going on when a Hispanic-looking guy attacked my men at Sweeney's shop, not long after you'd worked over the men I sent to Anita's house. I don't believe in coincidence. I began to connect the dots."

With an evil grin, Elaine strode over to stand in front of Luke. "I ordered Mendoza and his men to A.C. to wait for a large, important shipment. What better time to send you and Anita there? My computer geeks were trying to find evidence you were a Fed. If I learned you were, Mendoza would be close, ready to do to you what we did to Sweeney. What luck Ramon recognized you today. Saved me a lot of time and trouble. I've always had good luck. That's why I'm so successful." She released a chilling laugh. "*Your* luck just ran out."

Elaine whirled on Mendoza. "Show him we mean business."

"I want my turn with him," the guy who'd come in with Mace said.

"Don't worry, Gordon, you'll get your turn, but not the way you think." Elaine reached into the cross-body handbag she wore and pulled out a gun. Aiming it at Gordon, she said, "Did you really think I wouldn't find out you were the bastard who snitched to the FBI about that shipment at the Wilmington port? You cost me a lot of money."

Gordon's eyes widened. Sweat formed on his forehead. "That was payback. You shot my cousin." He turned and ran. Elaine shot him in the back. Before he hit the floor, she shot him in the head. He crumpled in a bloody heap.

At the cold-blooded way Elaine killed the guy, terror skittered over Anita's nerve endings.

Elaine looked around at the other men. "That's what happens to people who fail me." As calmly as a woman putting her lipstick away, she slipped her gun back into her purse and nodded to Mendoza.

"Lower him," Mendoza said to Ramon.

Ramon lowered Luke until his feet were inches from the ground.

Grinning, Mendoza fisted one beefy hand and punched Luke in the groin. Like a boxer with a punching bag, he swung again and again, hitting Luke in the stomach and chest.

"Go to hell," Luke spat out.

"You'll kill him," Anita screamed.

"That's the idea," Mendoza said with an evil grin.

Elaine strode back and forth in front of Anita and Luke, studying them, her gaze calculating.

"Let up for a while," she said to Mendoza. "We don't want him to die yet. He hasn't suffered enough."

Panic turned Anita's insides to mush. She'd never been in the presence of true evil before, although she'd always been uneasy around the Cutfords. Too bad she hadn't listened to her instincts.

Elaine went to Anita and yanked on her hair, forcing her head up. "I'm going to enjoy killing you. I've always been jealous of your looks, jealous that my husband has lusted after you for years. You won't be so pretty when we're done with you."

She slapped Anita across the face again. The metallic taste of blood filled Anita's mouth.

"Leave her alone," Luke cried out.

"You're a piece of scum, Elaine," Anita said, curling her lip. "I always knew there was something corrupt about you."

"Shut up, bitch!" Elaine slapped Anita again.

Anita's mouth hurt like hell, her head pounded, but she held her head high, refusing to show weakness. "How did you get involved with this group?" she said through swollen lips.

"Involved? Oh, that's rich." Elaine leaned closer. Anita read madness in the other woman's icy blue eyes.

"I *started* this 'group' as you call us," Elaine said. "You think we're a bridge club, you silly bitch? What was a poor, starving girl from Russia to do? My looks would fade one day and men would no longer pay for my body." She straightened and shrugged. "I had to figure out another way to support myself in the manner I deserved."

"We suspected the gang leader was Russian," Luke said, his words halting. "We didn't know you were a woman."

Elaine put a hand on her hip and faced Luke. "Being a woman made everything so much easier. Sweeney found out so we had to dispose of him. We're going to kill you, Corrado, and this little piece of fluff with you. You can go down easy or hard. Your choice. Tell us where the list is and your deaths will be quick."

Mace stepped forward and spoke to Elaine in a language Anita assumed was Russian. Elaine looked at Luke. "My husband reminds me he wants to fuck Anita, but that's not gonna happen. The other guys can have a go at her though."

"What the hell?" Mace screamed at Elaine. "You promised I could have her."

Elaine narrowed her eyes at her husband. "You don't like it? Leave. I made you, but I don't need you. I've got plenty of money and plenty of young studs hungry for the pleasures of my body. And for my money."

Looking down at the ground, Mace slunk back.

Luke struggled with his chains, his face contorted in pain. Anita suspected the movements only increased the tension on the chains. She looked up at Luke and tried to reassure him with her eyes that she didn't blame him for any of this. She couldn't blame anyone but the despicable ones holding them.

"I'm so sorry, sweetheart," Luke rasped.

"Isn't that sweet?" Elaine said. "They're in love."

The other men laughed.

Mendoza stepped forward and punched Luke in the groin again. Tied tight, Luke could only grunt.

"Tell us where the list is, bitch," Elaine said to Anita. "You continue this stubbornness and you'll suffer a lot more than rape."

"I don't know where the damn list is," Anita said. "Or even what it is."

"She's telling the truth," Luke said.

"Now, Luke, dear, lying is a sin." Elaine tapped one long, manicured fingernail against Luke's thigh. "We know the Feds don't have it yet, but you know where it is. Tell us, damn you! I'm losing patience."

Anita tried to free her hands from the zip ties. No use. If only she had the security training Jo did. She looked over at Luke. His gaze met hers. His eyes were darkened by pain, but he tried to smile. If they got out of this place alive, she'd tell him how much she loved him, and she'd never let him go. And she'd make him promise never to lie to her again.

Mace strode up to her and grabbed her by the shoulders, forcing her to her feet. She struggled to maintain her balance.

"I'm sick of waiting around," Mace said. "You tell us where the fucking list is, or you'll feel my fist."

"Real tough with everybody but your wife, huh, Mace? Screw you." Anita spat at him and struggled to free herself from his grip.

Mace threw her down onto the chair and pulled his hand back, prepared to strike her.

"Now, now, children, let's not fight." Elaine grabbed her husband's hand, stopping him. "Save it for later. We've got Corrado to deal with now." She nodded at Mendoza. "Give the Fed here a little taste of what's waiting for him. One of them, or both, knows where the list is. A little creative *interrogation* will get it out of them."

Mendoza pulled a knife from the waistband of his jeans. "Take him down," he said to Juan and Ramon. He held up the knife. "I've been waiting a long time for this, Corrado. I'm gonna cut your pretty face to shreds, then I'm gonna work lower. When they find your body, they won't know you were a man."

Juan and Ramon released Luke from the chains. His hands and feet were still tied. Luke staggered, and the men laughed. Suddenly, head forward, Luke lunged at Ramon, butting him in the stomach and sending him flying.

Juan tackled Luke. Anita flinched at the sound of Luke's head hitting the cement. Mace rushed to help Juan. They managed to subdue Luke and throw him into the chair. Luke slumped over.

With everyone's attention on Luke, Anita slowly began to stand. Maybe she could get outside. Maybe someone would see her and send help. She had to do something to save herself and Luke.

"Where the hell do you think you're going?" Elaine hissed. She grabbed Anita's hair and pulled hard. Pain shot through Anita but she defiantly met Elaine's gaze. Elaine pushed her back into the chair.

"Tell us where the list is," Mendoza said to Luke. Mendoza put the knife to Luke's neck, pricking the skin and drawing blood.

"You've killed him!" Anita screamed. White-hot anger boiled through her veins, giving her rage-fueled strength. She jumped from the chair and head-butted Elaine in the stomach. The other woman fell onto the floor. Anita fell on top of her. Fury overtook Anita, like a foreign entity invading her body. She knocked her forehead against Elaine's. Elaine pushed Anita away and jumped to her feet. Anita sprawled on the hard cement.

"You bitch!" Elaine screamed. She pulled her gun out of her purse and pointed it at Anita.

Anita closed her eyes and prayed. A gunshot rent the air. Anita felt no pain. Was this what death was like? She slowly opened her eyes and lifted her head. Elaine lay in a pool of blood next to her, her sightless eyes staring at the ceiling.

"Drop your weapons!" called a deep male voice. "Drop them!"

Anita squinted toward the door. Men wearing FBI jackets, guns drawn, followed by uniformed police, swarmed into the room.

Mace pulled a gun from the waistband of his pants and fired at the police. He turned and ran for the side door. Mendoza dropped his knife and followed Mace, the other men at his heels.

Shots rang out. Screaming in pain, Mace held onto his side and continued running. Another shot, and he went down. Juan and Ramon threw down their guns, held up their arms in surrender, and turned around. Mendoza made it to the door. A shot to his leg brought him down.

Paramedics rushed in. Some went to Anita and others to Luke and the men. An Agent helped Anita stand, motioning to one of the cops to free her. Anita rubbed her wrists, shook the paramedics aside and ran to Luke, who was still unconscious. Other paramedics were trying to revive him.

She knelt by his side, careful not to interfere. Stroking his cheek, she pushed down her rising fear. "Don't you dare die on me, Luke Corrado. I haven't given you hell yet for lying to me."

A burly FBI agent stood on Luke's other side. The guy's gaze met Anita's and he shook his head.

Fear choked her and she couldn't breathe. "No," she whispered. "No."

With a low groan, Luke slowly opened his eyes. Blinking, he looked at the guy standing next to him. "What took you so long, Murray?" he croaked out.

Luke turned his head slowly to face Anita. "I'm not going anywhere, sweetheart."

He passed out again.

CHAPTER TWENTY-THREE

Anita and Luke were transported to the hospital in separate ambulances. When they arrived, Jo and Franco were already waiting, along with Harris. Jo rushed up to Anita as they wheeled her, still on a stretcher, into an examination room. "God, Anita, we were so worried."

Franco, concern etched on his face, looked down at her. "Damn, cuz, you gave us a scare."

"I'll be okay," Anita said. "I'm not sure about Luke. They worked him over pretty good and he hit his head on the cement. I need to make sure he's all right." She tried to sit up.

Jo gently pushed her back down. "He's being cared for. We need to get you taken care of."

Anita slid her gaze between Jo and Franco. "What about you two? Are you okay?"

The couple looked at each other. "We're fine," Franco finally answered. "Now. When the FBI showed up at our door, we were a tad surprised."

Harris laughed. "Surprised is the understatement of the year. I'd stopped by to drop off some papers when the FBI came knocking."

"Was the list everyone wanted hidden in the jewel box I gave you?" Anita asked.

Harris nodded. "They found the list in a hidden compartment."

Anita grabbed Jo's hand. "I'm so sorry. I could have gotten you hurt or even killed."

"You didn't know about any of this," Jo said. "The FBI has

the list, the bad guys are put away, and we're all okay."

Anita tried to smile, but her face hurt too much. "When I'm sure Luke will be all right, I'm giving him hell for lying to me."

"Go easy on him," Franco said. "He had good reasons for lying."

"The police raid is all over the news," Harris said to Anita. "You and Luke are being hailed as heroes."

"We're hardly that."

Franco shook his head. "I still can't believe Elaine Cutford was the leader of that gang. There was always something about her that creeped me out."

A man wearing scrubs and holding a clipboard came into the room. "I'm Dr. Morgan. I need to ask all of you to leave while I examine the patient."

◇◇◇

Her injuries taken care of, Anita was held overnight for observation and released the next day. She had a wicked bruise on her jaw and her cut lip throbbed, but otherwise she was okay. Jo and Franco insisted on taking her back to their house.

"I need to see Luke first," Anita said when she was ready to leave. She went to his room alone, leaving the others to wait for her in the hospital cafeteria. When she got to Luke's room, one of the cops guarding it refused to let her enter. "No one's allowed in there, ma'am."

"You're going to let me in," she said, more loudly than she'd intended.

The door opened and the man Luke had called Murray stuck his head out. "What's going on?"

The cop jerked his thumb at Anita. "She wants to go in."

"It's okay." Murray smiled at Anita and stepped back. "Go in. He's asking for you."

"Thank you," she said. "For everything." She frowned. "I've been wondering. How did you and your men know where to find us?"

He laughed. "Corrado has a tracker he slips into a hidden pocket in his jeans. We always have a backup, knowing the phones will get destroyed."

"Good insurance."

"Go in. Your man is waiting for you."

She entered the room and Murray closed the door behind her, leaving her alone with Luke.

Anita walked in cautiously. When she saw Luke, she suppressed a cry, putting a hand over her mouth. He sat propped up on pillows. His wrists where he'd been chained were bandaged. His nose and eyes were swollen. Bruises marred his strong jaw.

"You look like hell," she said, forcing a smile.

"You should see the other guy," he said in a raspy voice. He tried to smile, but winced instead.

She touched his hand and sniffed.

"You crying for me?" he asked.

"Yes."

"No one's cried for me in a very long time."

Trying to lighten the atmosphere, she said, "Enjoy it now, buster, because after you're healed, we need to have a long talk."

"I know. I only ask that you give me a chance to make things right."

"Luke, you know how I feel about guys who lie. I understand why you had to hide things from me, but I've got some baggage left over from Kent and it's hard to let go of something I've carried around for a long time." She smiled. "But I'm trying."

He squeezed her hand. "I hated lying to you, sweetheart, but I couldn't compromise the investigation. Please forgive me."

"After all we've been through, there's nothing to forgive. We're alive and we're together."

◇◇◇

Five days had passed since Luke and Anita were abducted and the criminals arrested. With Elaine dead, her gang in custody, and the list secured by the FBI, Anita no longer feared for her life.

But she feared for her future, one without Luke. She loved him with a fever she never thought possible. Did he want a life with her?

As she walked out to her car to drive to the hospital to get Luke, who was being released that day, she wondered if today would be the end, if she was merely a case to him and he'd move on to another one. She rubbed the back of her neck to release the tense muscles. She hadn't had a good night's sleep since before Atlantic City.

She'd spent every day since her release with Luke. They still hadn't talked about their future or if they had one together. Justin took care of her salon and her customers so she was free to heal herself, inside and out, and to focus on Luke.

Later, she helped him up the steps to her loft. The FBI had cleaned out the loft they'd leased for him and it was up for rent again. Snow had begun falling and she knew the steps and side-walks would get icy. She and Luke would be safe and secure inside and together.

"I can walk fine," he said.

She continued to hold onto his arm. "You were badly injured. I'm not letting go of you." *I never want to let go of you*, she wanted to say. She bit back the words. It wasn't time yet.

They entered her place and Luke headed straight for the sofa. He sank down on the cushions and leaned back, his eyes closed. His usually bronzed skin was pale, and sweat beaded his forehead.

Anita's heart thumped so loudly, she was sure he could hear it in the quiet room. "Would you like some tea?" she asked.

He opened his eyes and sat straighter. "Later." He patted the seat next to him. "Come here. We need to talk."

Swallowing her anxiety, she sat next to him, folding her hands primly on her lap. "You first. I want to know all about you, and I want to hear about Mexico, Maria, and your son."

Luke smoothed his hand over his hair. His gaze locked with hers. "I joined the FBI right out of college. For most of the last five years I've been deep undercover trying to break up Elaine's cartel." He shook his head. "I've seen a lot in my work, but a woman as hard-core as Elaine? That's a first."

"Is she really from Russia?"

He nodded. "She was clever, invented a new background for herself, down to fake documents that were posted on government sites by her computer hackers. When the Agency checked into her, there was no evidence she was born in Russia." He shot Anita a wry smile. "She'd even perfected a Philadelphia accent. The woman missed her calling as an actress."

"She sure had me fooled, but my instincts told me not to trust her. I should have listened."

"Don't beat yourself up over it, sweetheart. She fooled a lot of people."

"You were undercover in Mexico?" Anita asked.

He settled into his seat and closed his eyes for a few seconds, and Anita wondered if he was picturing his dangerous time there.

Luke opened his eyes, but he didn't look at her. Instead, he stared across the room. "We'd gotten good intel that Mendoza was one of the most powerful men in the human trafficking ring. He also had ties to a vicious drug cartel in Mexico. Using the name Luis Correa, I went to Mexico and passed myself off as a drug dealer in the Southwest United States interested in expanding my operations. I got in deep with Mendoza and his men. They trusted me. I met his sister, Maria." Luke turned to Anita. "We fell in love."

When he mentioned Maria, his voice softened. Needing fortification to hear about the woman Luke had loved, maybe still loved, Anita stood. "I could use some wine. Anything for you?"

"Water, please."

When she'd gotten their drinks and was seated again, she said, "Tell me about Maria."

Luke held the large water goblet between his hands, as if he needed to cling to something. Staring straight ahead, he said, "Our affair was hot and heavy. Because she feared her brother, we kept it secret. She was a virgin when I met her, and Mendoza was very protective. We found out why he was so protective of her."

Luke turned to Anita, disgust on his face. "Mendoza planned to sell Maria to the highest bidder." Luke took a large swig of water. "He had a lot of contacts in Russia. Seems some of those men are willing to pay a lot for a young virgin.

"The Agency thought one of Mendoza's Russian contacts might be the leader of the human trafficking ring, the one we'd been looking for," he continued. "But Sweeney, using different intel, learned the leader was in Philly. The Agency sent Sweeney to Philly and used the antique shop as a front. Sweeney's parents owned an antique shop in Ohio so it was a good cover. Our street contacts spread the word that Sweeney would be willing to use his shop to launder money and that he was into some sick shit, like child porn. And human trafficking."

Anita shivered.

"It worked," Luke said. "Sweeney got in with the local trafficking crowd. But he still didn't know who the leader was."

"How did the list come into all this?" Anita sipped her wine and watched Luke.

"Just before Sweeney disappeared, he got wind of a list that contained the names of agents, both U.S. and foreign, working in Eastern Europe. The list also had the dates and places for several shipments of women and children who were victims."

Anita put a hand to her stomach. "If Elaine and her crowd had gotten hold of that list, all those agents would be dead, and those women and children wouldn't have a chance. Oh, Luke, how terrible, for everyone."

"Yeah, it was, but thankfully that won't happen now. Near as we can figure out, Sweeney must have gotten hold of the list, and thinking the gang was onto him, he stuck the list in the jewel box and gave it to you. Maybe he thought he could come back for it."

Chills ran over Anita, and she set down her wine glass and moved closer to Luke, seeking his warmth. "Poor Sweeney. He really was a nice man."

"He was one of the best." Luke put down his water goblet, took her hand, and held it on his lap. His gaze locked with hers.

"When we didn't find the list at his shop or in any of his personal accounts, we figured he'd given it to you. The crime ring figured the same thing. Under questioning, Mace admitted Sweeney had said your name before he died."

She swallowed, her throat too thick to speak.

Anita drew a calming breath and grabbed her glass, finishing off the wine. "What happened to Maria?" she finally managed.

Luke's features tensed and his lips thinned into a harsh line. "She died because I was too hotheaded to follow orders."

"What?"

"When Mendoza got word I might be a Fed, he and some of his men captured and tortured me, but Murray and his guys rescued me. I had to flee Mexico. I couldn't take Maria then. I wanted to go back for her, but I was ordered to stay out of Mexico. And since we had what we thought was a strong lead in Los Angeles, I was sent there."

His Adam's apple worked as he talked, and he looked away. "When the lead in L.A. didn't pan out, the Agency gave me back my personal cell phone. There were frantic voicemails from Maria begging me to come for her."

His jaw tensed, and he continued. "When I was forced to leave the first time, I thought she'd be safe until I could go back for her. I didn't know she was pregnant. I should have gone sooner. I should never have left her."

Anita put her hand over his. "You had a duty to your country, and you thought she'd be okay."

"Maybe, but that doesn't stop my guilt. Murray refused to give me the okay to go back to Mexico."

"So you went anyway."

He nodded. "I met Maria at the small cabin in the mountains where we used to go. Her bags were packed, and she told me we had to pick up someone else on our way out of the country. I figured it was Adelina, the elderly woman who was like a grandmother to her. I know now she wanted to take me to Miguel, our son. She never got that chance. I've been wondering why she didn't tell me then that we had a son, but maybe she wanted to be sure we were free from Mendoza."

Luke turned to Anita, his eyes haunted. "As we were leaving, Mendoza showed up. One of his spies told him Maria had contacted me and I was on the way back to Mexico."

Rubbing a hand down his face, Luke said, "He shot Maria in front of me. She died in my arms." His voice thickened and he stared down at the table, quiet for a few minutes as if trying to compose himself. When he started talking again, he didn't look at Anita. "Mendoza and his guys took me prisoner and worked me over, but the FBI and the Mexican police got there before Mendoza could finish me off."

"Oh, Luke, I'm so sorry." She touched his face until he turned to her. "What about your son? Where is he?"

"Here in Philly. I found out about him a short while ago when Adelina called me. Our men brought him back from Mexico before Christmas. Mendoza wanted to kill Miguel."

"My God, how awful. What an evil man." Anita framed Luke's face between her hands. "You have a son to think about now. The past is over. Who is looking after Miguel?"

"Social services placed him with a foster family. I've seen him once and have talked to the family by phone. He'll slowly get to know me before I take custody."

"Oh, Luke." She released him, but sidled closer.

"I have a son who doesn't know me, and the woman I'd loved was killed because I disobeyed orders. If I hadn't gone to Mexico, Maria might still be alive."

An ache formed in Anita's throat. She took Luke's hand in hers, stroking the smooth skin, wishing she could do more to dissolve his pain.

"I killed Maria just as surely as if I'd pulled the trigger. And my son lost his mother."

Anita gathered Luke to her, holding him against her chest. "It's not your fault she died. You're a brave and honorable man."

As she held him, she felt him relax. Finally, she released him, but held onto his hand. "Your tattoo—the cross and dagger.

It has something to do with all this, doesn't it?"

"It's to remind me that evil walks among the good. I've seen things that haunt me, done things I'm not proud of."

"But you helped a lot of people."

He kissed her lightly on the lips. "You're too good for me. I know our relationship began with a deception. Can we start over? I need you in my life. You've made me feel whole again. From the first, you've tempted me to open my heart, to dream of a future I thought lost."

Her heartbeat drummed in her ears. Her old fears reared up, but so did hope, something she hadn't felt for a long time. Focusing on a spot on the wall across from them, she carefully chose her words. "I've been thinking a lot about us the past week. Since Kent, I've kept my heart and my feelings locked away, determined never to let another man hurt me or lie to me. I had to be the one in control, the one who walked away from relationships."

"And how do you feel now?" he asked quietly.

She faced him. "I'm afraid of my feelings for you, Luke. I want to run and hide, to protect myself." She bit down on her lip. "But I can't let you walk out of my life. Let's take our time and see where this goes."

His features softened. "I'm not sure what's going to happen with my job. And I have a son to consider. But I do know one thing for certain."

She forced air into her lungs. "What?"

"I love you, Anita Santisi, more than I've ever loved anyone. Can you learn to love me?"

Like the sun bursting through clouds, joy filled her. "Learn to love you? I think I fell in love with you that first night, when I ran down my steps and into your arms. I never thought I'd love someone the way I love you."

He wiped a tear from her face with his thumb. Wonder shone from his eyes. "You love me?"

She could only nod.

His smile lit his face and showed that dimple she loved so

much. He sobered. "I'm not perfect. I've done things--"

She put a finger over his mouth. "Shut up and kiss me."

"Anita," he whispered, sealing their love with a kiss.

<><><>

Two months later

Anita grabbed Luke's arm and pulled him to a stop. Pedestrians pushed by them on the street in one of Philadelphia's gentrified neighborhoods. She moved to avoid the foot traffic and met Luke's gaze. "What if Miguel doesn't like me?"

"He'll love you as I love you."

"This might be too much for the poor little boy. He's just gotten to know and accept you. Now you bring me into his life."

Luke grasped her arms. "Adelina raised him and he loved her. It was men he didn't trust. He'll love you. How could he not?"

Freeing herself, Anita sighed and pressed her arms against her midriff. In the past months, Luke had taken a desk job at the Philadelphia field office and moved into her loft. He'd visited his son every day, each time spending a little longer with him. Miguel had gradually begun to accept Luke. In a week, Luke would take Miguel home to live with him and Anita.

She dropped her arms to her sides and released a breath. "Okay. Let's do this."

"That's my Anita." Luke took her hand, and together they climbed the steps to the townhouse. Before Luke could ring the bell, the door opened, and a woman stood there, a smile on her face.

"Come in. He is waiting for you."

When they entered the living room, a little black-haired boy, the image of Luke, screamed, "Papi." He ran to Luke and flung himself into his arms.

Joy on his face, Luke lifted his son and hugged him close. Miguel wrapped his arms around Luke's neck and said something in Spanish.

"English, Miguel," Luke said.

"Home, Papi."

Luke turned to face Anita. "Miguel, this is my friend Anita." Luke spoke slowly, enunciating each word.

Miguel looked at Anita with big brown eyes, Luke's eyes. Her heart swelled and her throat thickened. She instantly fell in love. Every maternal instinct she possessed coalesced to embrace this little boy. Ready to hold him, she raised her arms. Reluctantly, she lowered them, knowing she had to take it easy with him.

"Hello, Miguel," she said in as soft a voice as she could. "I hope you and I can be good friends."

Miguel blinked. He gave her a shy smile before he buried his head in his father's neck.

Luke, his eyes moist, met Anita's gaze over the boy's head. "Give him time."

A tear slipped down her cheek. "Of course, I'll give him time. He belongs to both of us now."

Still holding his son, Luke stepped closer. "Anita, from the first, you've tempted me with the possibility of hope, of love, of healing. You've made me happier than I ever thought possible."

"Oh, Luke." Her heart felt ready to burst.

"Will you marry us?" Luke asked.

She licked her suddenly dry lips and swallowed around the lump in her throat. "Yes, my love, yes."

Still holding his son, Luke embraced her. They clung to each other, the three of them, a family.

EPILOGUE

Two years later

Anita kissed six-month old Sofia Maria's forehead and lay the sleeping infant in the portable crib in the guest room at Logan and Doriana's house in Tucson. Anita sank onto the upholstered chair next to the crib to take a much-needed rest. With the whole family visiting for Christmas, things could get a little hectic.

Things might be hectic, she thought, smiling, but she wouldn't have it any other way. Jo and Franco were there with two-year-old Josey. All three of Logan and Doriana's kids—twenty-three-year-old Josh, six-year-old Lena Marie, and two-and-a half year old Danny—were at the house. Aunt Lena and Uncle Dan, along with her beloved Nonna, were there too.

Anita sighed. Life was good. Married and with a family, Luke hadn't wanted to do undercover work. He'd recently gotten a promotion to director of the Los Angeles field office. After the holidays, they'd travel there to house hunt. With her Philadelphia loft on the market and her salon sold to Justin, she was free to devote herself to her family.

Anita stood and kissed Sofia Maria again and tiptoed out of the room. As she closed the door behind her, she heard footsteps. Luke and Miguel came down the hall. When Miguel, almost five now, saw her, he dropped his father's hand and ran to Anita.

"Mama!" He held up his arms.

Anita bent and gave him a tight hug. Straightening, she took the little boy's hand. She couldn't love Miguel more if she'd given birth to him.

◇◇◇

His heart filled to overflowing with love, Luke kissed his wife on the cheek. "We got worried about you. You were gone so long."

"It took a little longer than normal to settle Sofia Maria."

"I want to see Sofia," Miguel said, pointing to the closed bedroom door.

"You can see your sister later, after she's had her nap," Luke said. "Come on, let's go join the rest of the family."

He took Miguel's hand.

As they walked, their son between them, Luke looked over at Anita. "I love you more every day. At one time, I wasn't sure God existed, but now I know He does. He sent you to me."

"And you to me," she said in a thick voice.

Anita. His wonderful temptation, the woman he'd been waiting for. His life had come full circle. He finally had what he'd always wanted—love and a family of his own.

Thank you for reading *Luke's Temptation*. Please enjoy an excerpt from Cara Marsi's *Murder, Mi Amore*

MURDER, MI AMORE
BY
CARA MARSI

CHAPTER ONE

A prickly sensation, like someone breathing on the back of her neck, sent chills slithering down Lexie Cortese's spine. She glanced around the small, exclusive leather goods shop on one of Rome's busiest streets. A well-dressed older woman perused a richly sequined evening bag while a smiling saleswoman looked on. A middle-aged man, dressed in a beautifully tailored gray suit, studied a display case of couture handbags. Nothing sinister. Yet the feeling of being followed had started before she'd entered the shop and had grown stronger in the forty-five minutes she'd been there.

"*Signorina? Carta di credito?*"

Lexie started at the saleswoman's words and turned back to her with an apologetic smile. Although she couldn't speak Italian, Lexie had done enough shopping to know the saleswoman wanted her credit card. She dug into her plain black shoulder bag, pushing aside the bright scarf she'd tied on the handle to liven it up a bit, pulled out her card and handed it to the woman. As she waited for the clerk to ring up the sale, someone jostled her.

"*Scusi, per favore.*" The middle-aged man in the gray suit had bumped her. His flat black eyes bore into hers, as if sending her a message. She backed away.

"No *problema*," she said, hoping she had the Italian right.

With a cold smile, he moved on, heading to the door.

Clutching her shopping bag with one hand and holding her shoulder bag tightly against her, she left the shop and joined the throngs of pedestrians on the Via Corsi. Despite the festive atmosphere from shoppers and tourists enjoying an unseasonably warm April day, Lexie couldn't shake the feeling that someone followed her.

Was it the man who'd bumped into her, the one with the dead eyes? She shouldered her way along the crowded street and looked behind her. He wasn't there. God, she was becoming paranoid, letting her imagination run amok. Nevertheless, she tightened her grip on the shopping bag that contained the way-too-expensive dark green designer handbag she'd just purchased. Rome was as well-known for its pickpockets and muggers as for its art and history.

Why would anyone follow her, an ordinary tourist? Then again, she wasn't ordinary any more. Not since she'd come to Rome. And now she had a new handbag to go with her new attitude. In the past two weeks, the cautious, always-do-what's-right-eager-to-please-everyone Lexie Cortese had become a confident, take-charge woman. For all of her twenty-eight years she'd done what others wanted—her parents, her teachers, that louse Jerry. But no more.

Smiling at a vendor selling flowers, she inhaled the heady perfume of early spring blooms and put a little bounce in her step. A good-looking twenty-something man nodded to her as he passed. Lots of handsome Italian men had flirted with her in the two weeks she'd been here. Sure helped make up for what that scum of an ex-fiancé had done.

From now on she'd do whatever she damn well pleased. Spend a month in Rome? Check. Buy a designer bag that cost more than a month's pay? Done. Have a fling with a sexy Italian, then walk away, in control, her heart untouched? Not so sure about that one, but she could hope.

To celebrate the new Lexie, she'd have a glass of wine. Maybe even two glasses. The Trevi Fountain was close. She'd enjoy her drink in the popular piazza admiring old Neptune and his trident. The prickly feeling swept over her again, raising goose bumps on her arms. She stopped and scanned the street. Nothing. Damn it!

Her imagination was in overdrive. It had to be. Thirsty for some calming wine, she hurried toward the piazza.

She found a seat at one of the outdoor tables directly across from old Neptune and ordered a glass of Pinot Noir. The piazza buzzed with tourists snapping pictures and throwing their three coins in the famous fountain. She'd made her three wishes the day she'd arrived. Wish one—that she'd find success in her new job and in grad school; wish two—that she'd come back to Rome, maybe even study here; and three—that someday she'd find real love and happiness. Whatever real happiness was.

When her wine arrived, she held the glass up in salute to Neptune. *Okay, water boy, do your stuff. Grant my wishes and toss a little excitement my way.* With a smile, she took a sip. The rich liquid flowed down her throat, soothing her jumbled nerves. How foolish she'd been to feel so unsettled earlier. Maybe traces of the old, skittish Lexie lingered.

A movement from a side street near the fountain snagged her attention. A man wearing jeans and a hoodie shot from the street, running directly toward…

Her?

Lexie gasped and grabbed her purse from the tabletop as the man raced past and snatched her shopping bag from the ground next to her.

"Hey!" Lexie jumped to her feet. "That's mine!"

The man ignored her, clutching the bag with her new, expensive purse against his chest like a football as he sprinted down a small alleyway.

"Somebody stop him!" she shouted, knocking over the table. The wine goblet shattered onto the cobblestones, splattering red wine all over her black sandals.

The piazza erupted in cries and frantic calls for the police. Onlookers, yelling in several languages, pointed toward the narrow street where the thief had disappeared. Several men ran after him. Lexie started to follow them.

"Stay, *signorina*," her waiter implored, grabbing her arm and holding her back. His eyes, wide and stricken, darted from her to the piazza. "See. The police. They are coming." He pointed out two policemen racing toward the alleyway. "Please, *signorina*, sit, have some wine. No charge." He pulled out a chair at a freshly made up table. Another waiter stood close, holding a full glass of wine out to Lexie.

Reluctantly, she turned away from the chase. "Thank you." She sank into the chair and took the proffered wine, grasping the glass tightly to control her sudden trembling as she noticed people staring.

Damn it all to hell! That purse was supposed to symbolize her new attitude. And now some scumbag had stolen it not ten minutes after she walked out of the store with it. What did that say about her chances for a new start?

She looked up to see strangers hovering, offering help in a scattering of languages. She tried to respond, to reassure them she was all right. Her bout of self-pity dissolved with the strangers' kindness. She could handle this.

Fifteen long minutes later, her wine untouched, Lexie stared dismally across the piazza in the direction the thief and his pursuers had taken. Her waiters stood nearby, their faces tense.

"The police will find him, *signorina*. They must."

Then, like ancient Roman warriors returning from battle, the two policemen, followed by a large group of raucous men and boys, materialized from the alleyway. A tall man wearing a suit and holding her shopping bag walked between the policemen. Who was he? Not the thief.

She stood as they approached, wishing she knew enough Italian to ask. His well-cut, dark blue business suit emphasized his broad shoulders and muscular frame as he strode across the piazza toward her. His thick, wavy black hair was expertly slicked back from a face boasting razor sharp cheekbones and a strong jaw. He might as well have jumped from the pages of a men's fashion magazine into her Roman holiday.

"*Signorina*," Mr. GQ Cover Model said, smiling and holding her bag out to her. He said something totally incomprehensible in Italian, and when she simply stared, he arched one dark eyebrow and tried again. "I believe this is yours?"

His English, spoken with a lilting Italian accent, sent unexpected spasms of pleasure over her. Unwilling to tear her gaze away from that oh-so-charming smile, Lexie stalled. She'd never seen a man so ruggedly beautiful.

She'd been without sex for too long. That was the only explanation.

"*Grazie*," she finally said, taking the bag from him. She opened the bag to make sure her purse was indeed inside, then smiled up at her handsome knight. "Thank you so much. You could have been hurt going after that jerk."

He lifted one elegantly-clad shoulder. "It was nothing. Vermin like that give my city a bad name." He studied her. "You are American." Surprise edged his deep, rich voice.

She nodded, then turned to the policemen, who stood silently by. How odd. "*Grazie* to both of you too."

They touched the brims of their hats at the same time. "We did nothing," the older of the two said. "This gentleman had wrestled your bag from the thief before we got there."

"Where is the thief?" Lexie asked, glancing around.

The policeman shrugged. "He got away, but be assured, we will find him." He smiled and pulled a small notebook from his inside jacket pocket. "Please to give us a little information for our report."

"Of course," she said. She quickly gave them the information they wanted.

"Thank you, *signorina*," the policeman said as he snapped his notebook shut and stuffed it back into his pocket. His partner remained silent and she assumed he didn't speak English. With nods to her, the policemen left.

"Thanks again," Lexie called after them.

She turned to the handsome stranger who'd rescued her bag. "Please, let me buy you a drink as thanks for your help."

"Of course. How can I refuse an invitation from such a beautiful woman?"

Lexie blushed. Italian men sure knew how to make a woman feel sexy. She turned back to her table where her waiter stood waiting. With a smile of gratitude, she slid into the chair he held for her. She put her purse and shopping bag under the table, on the side closest to the wall. Mr. GQ Cover Model sat in the opposite chair and ordered a glass of Pinot Noir in beautiful Italian.

"I'm Lexie Cortese," she said, holding out her hand to shake his.

He took her hand and turned it over, brushing his lips on her wrist. Sparks seemed to fly up her arm and she felt her eyes widen. *This man could charm Neptune's nymphs right out of the fountain.*

Trying her best not to blush again, she smiled and pulled her hand free.

"Domenico Brioni," he said, gifting her with a melt-her-bones smile. Despite his overt sexuality, humor flashed in his eyes, as if he didn't quite take himself seriously. "My American friends call me Dominic."

Oh, yes, she definitely could get used to this. "I hope we can be friends so I shall call you Dominic." The old Lexie would never be so bold with a man she'd just met.

"Of course, we will be friends," he said with another of his smiles. "Cortese. Italian?"

"My great-grandparents came from Abruzzo."

"Abruzzo. That explains your beautiful hazel eyes."

He was a practiced charmer all right. But she liked it.

"Do you speak Italian?" he asked.

"I don't, I'm sorry to say. But you speak beautiful English."

His eyes sparkled with even greater good humor. "Thank you." When the waiter handed him his wine, he held up his glass to her in salute.

Two hours and two glasses of wine later as he walked her back to her hotel—to make sure she arrived safely he'd insisted—she realized she'd done most of the talking. She'd told him about her home in Las Vegas, her new job at the college, her plan to some day earn a doctorate in Ancient Roman studies.

But she didn't tell him about Jerry. She was growing. She was healing.

Her life was far from exciting, yet Dominic continued to listen to her as if she were fascinating. A little niggle of doubt arose as she realized he'd told her very little about himself, only that he was a native Roman who worked in the banking business.

"I would like to see you again, Lexie Cortese," he said when they reached her hotel. His gaze, as warm as the heat of the sun that had made her feel so relaxed and content in the piazza, now sparked another kind of heat in her. When he brushed back a strand of hair from her forehead, jolts of electricity shot to every part of her body. The man had magic in those fingers.

Lexie had always been fond of magic shows.

"I'd love to see you again too," she said, tilting her face up to look at him. He was tall for an Italian, towering over her by about a foot.

He smiled. "It's a date. Dinner tomorrow night?"

"Uh-huh," she said, her mind and her body filled with his smile.

"I will pick you up here at eight," he said.

God, he was gorgeous. Could she put aside a lifetime of caution and take a chance on him? "Eight is good."

He took her hand and kissed her knuckles. "*Buon giorno*, Lexie Cortese. Until tomorrow."

****

*I hope you enjoyed this excerpt of *Murder, Mi Amore* by Cara Marsi. If you'd like to read the book in its entirety, please check with your favorite online retailer for availability, or visit Cara's website at CaraMarsi.com for purchase info.*

BOOKS BY CARA MARSI

A Catered Romance
A Cat's Tale & Other Love Stories
(All stories in this anthology are available separately)
A Cinderella Christmas
A Groom for Christmas
Accidental Love
Cursed Mates
Her Forever Husband
Her Snow White Christmas (Snow Globe Magic Book 1)
Logan's Redemption (Redemption Book 1)
Franco's Fortune (Redemption Book 2)
Luke's Temptation (Redemption Book 3)
Love Potion
Loving Or Nothing
Murder, Mi Amore
Storm of Desire
Sweet Temptations
Sweet Temptations Boxed Set
The One Who Got Away
The Marriage Coin (Anthology)
The Ring
Wedding Dreams Boxed Set

Coming 2015, Capri Nights
Also Coming 2015, Her Frog Prince Holiday (Snow Globe Magic Book 2)

Read excerpts at www.caramarsi.com
All books available at online booksellers
A Catered Romance, A Groom for Christmas, Franco's Fortune, Logan's Redemption, Loving Or Nothing, Luke's Temptation, and Murder, Mi Amore are also available in print
***

An award-winning and eclectic author, Cara Marsi is published in romantic suspense, paranormal romance, and contemporary romance. She loves a good love story, and believes that everyone deserves a second chance at love. Sexy, sweet, thrilling, or magical, Cara's stories are first and foremost about the love. Treat yourself today, with a taste of romance. When not traveling or dreaming of traveling, Cara and her husband live on the East Coast in a house ruled by two spoiled cats who compete for attention.

Find out more about Cara and her books and sign up for her newsletter at her website at CaraMarsi.com. She's on Twitter, Goodreads, Facebook, and Pinterest and is always interested in meeting new friends.

***

www.ingramcontent.com/pod-product-compliance
Lightning Source LLC
Chambersburg PA
CBHW061208170626
46809CB00003B/1290